# The Real Sedro-Woolley

and other imaginings of the Pacific Northwest

Robert McLean

Table of contents

Imagining #1: The Real Sedro-Woolley          p. 1

Imagining #2: The Time Capsule                p. 85

Imagining #3: Twelve Pies                     p. 95

Imagining #4: Wolves                          p. 105

Imagining #5: Glacier, WA                     p. 109

# Imagining #1: The Real Sedro-Woolley

## Chapter 1: Discovered

Every story needs to start somewhere. I'll start this one with something that happened in school the first week of September, though it's kind of trivial and it's not really when things started. Our English teacher gave us an in-class assignment where we had to write about what we want to be when we grow up. Before we could start writing, he had us discuss the question out loud – 'brainstorming' he calls it. There's this one kid in my class who's generally a real space cadet, and he immediately blurted out,

"I want to be famous."

Most of the time the space cadet (his actual name is Lucas, though no one except teachers calls him by it) gets laughed at by the other kids whenever he speaks in class because he can be so darn weird. For example, back in ninth grade the math teacher once asked the class to describe a pentagon. The space cadet put up his hand and started to give a long description of the Pentagon Building in Washington DC, where the US military headquarters is, and how close it came to being destroyed by the 9/11 terrorists, and then he got really pissed off when the teacher interrupted him and said,

"Just describe the shape, Lucas."

The teacher had to ask someone else to answer. But the space cadet kept trying to interrupt the next kid so he could explain how 9/11 was a government conspiracy, and finally the teacher had to tell him to leave the room. But this time the other kids in class were nodding in agreement, because for once he said something sensible. The teacher asked him,

"Famous for what, Lucas?"

to which the space cadet replied,

"I don't know, for something, I guess. I'm just hoping to get discovered."

More nodding. The other kids were all thinking the same thing, they want to be discovered, too, each one of them an America waiting for its Christopher Columbus to come along. Me, I was thinking, give me a fucking break. Only I didn't just think it, I muttered it out loud,

"Give me a fucking break."

Fortunately I was sitting near the back of the classroom, so the teacher didn't hear exactly what I said. But he knew I must have said something out of the ordinary, since everyone sitting near me turned their heads and stared.

"Did you have something you wanted to add, Landon?"

the teacher asked. To which I replied,

"I said, 'I thinks that's really great'. Space Ca... I mean, Lucas, has a really unique outlook on things. I don't always agree with what he says, but it's always interesting. Maybe he'll be on the TV news one day, offering alternative viewpoints on current events"

As you can see, I can think pretty quick on my feet when I need to. The teacher bought it, and moved on with the brainstorming session, while I returned to my previous thought. Which was, who gives a shit about being famous? I certainly don't. I don't care whether anyone discovers me or not. I'm more interested in doing some discovering of my own, if you know what I mean. I want to discover what it's like to surf on the Pacific Ocean. I want to discover the feel of a carpet of douglas fir and redwood needles under my hiking boots. I'd like to discover the smell of the mountains in the hair of a girl I've spent an afternoon hiking with in the Cascades. I figure if you're busy discovering things like that, you won't care whether the rest of the world discovers you.

This whole "I want to be discovered" thing that the other kids in my school hope for is pretty sad. And I suspect there's a lot of people out there who think the same way, not just the people at my school. I blame TV. I read once that the internet and gaming was going to kill off TV, but most people I know still spend way too much time watching it. Especially those reality shows where a bunch of losers get drunk and fight with each other and the guys call the girls 'bitches' and the girls call each other 'sluts' and shit like that. I'm sure you've seen them. Reality TV shows are like when a dog starts shitting on a lawn; once you see it, you can't stop yourself from watching until it's done. So my strategy for TV is the same one I use for shitting dogs: I avoid looking at it. That way I don't get hooked on reality shows, and don't waste any brain cells. But the other kids at my school can't help themselves, and it makes them dream that maybe one day TV cameras will show up on their doorsteps to make shows about them, too. Seriously. As if. What the other kids don't seem to realize that no one in the rest of the world gives a rat's ass about what anyone in this town does. I mean, seriously. Look at the photo on the cover of this book (not the trees, that's a forest out west. The houses). That's where I live. Would you want to watch a show about the people who live in that place? I don't think so. Nothing interesting ever happens here. It's like a sort of beige prison colony.

My name's Landon Go, by the way, and my hometown is... actually, I better not tell you the real name of my town. Not that you would remember it anyway, but some of the stuff I'm going to tell you about people around here isn't very flattering. If any of them figures out what I've written is about them, they might kill me or sue me. Or even more likely is that I'll write something that's about someone else, but they'll think it's about them and I'll get killed or sued anyway. So I've got to play it safe. I already have, starting by changing the space cadet's name, which isn't really Lucas.

Instead of telling you my town's real name, let me tell you where I'd like to live: Sedro-Woolley. Isn't that an unusual and supercool name for a place? I haven't been there yet, so I don't know for sure if the town really is as cool or unusual as its name. It's in Washington state, and I saw the name on a map. I've never been to Washington state either, but I have no doubt it is totally cool. Most things that are cool originate in the West, like organic food, Ansel Adams photos, grunge music, longboards, and good coffee. And of course, there's the mountains and redwood forests and coastline, none of which we have where I presently live. My life goal is to strike out for the real Sedro-Woolley when I'm old enough and I've got all my shit together. So in answer to the English teacher's start-of-semester assignment about what I'm going to do when I grow up, I wrote simply two words: Go west.

Since I'm going to be stuck here for a few years yet, let me tell you a bit more about my hometown of Not-Sedro-Woolley. Fifty-one thousand people live here, not one of them famous. That's roughly five times more people than live in the real Sedro-Woolley, which has a population of ten thousand, six hundred and thirty-six according to the latest US Census. The Census happens every ten years, it's when the government counts every person in the country and asks them questions like how old they are, what their job is, and stuff like that. The first US Census was organized by Thomas Jefferson, who is one of the four presidents on Mount Rushmore (I haven't been there, either). Jefferson's not my favorite Rushmore president – that would be Teddy Roosevelt – but the fact Jefferson was chosen for Rushmore shows you that he was a pretty big deal. Jefferson was a Founding Father of the US, and helped write the Declaration of Independence, but I bet organizing the first census was a lot harder. I mean, it took our homeroom teacher ages to take attendance on the first day of class because so many of the students (mostly the guys) were messing around. Could you imagine trying to take attendance for the whole country?

Especially back in the days before computers were invented, and a lot of people couldn't even write their own names?

Not-Sedro-Woolley is over 200 years old. Our main tourist attraction is a park that has a museum of log buildings built by the first white settlers. There was an Indian settlement here for thousands of years, but when the settlers arrived they kicked the Indians off the land and shipped them to a reservation five hundred miles from here. That sort of thing happened all over North America 200 years ago. I'm sorry if you don't like to hear how our Founding Fathers were a bunch of land thieves, but that's the truth, and in my view it's best to tell the truth about the past, even if it's an ugly truth.

That's one reason why I get so bored in history class. The history they teach you in school is mostly fiction, and not very interesting fiction at that. I mean, last month our history teacher stood there at the front of the class and told us how the first settlers came here and tamed the wild and planted crops and bravely worked to build a great community and if they were still around today we'd call them 'heroes' and blah, blah, blah. He said not word about the Indians who were here first, or what happened to them. The following day we got out of school and took a field trip to the museum. It totally sucked. I hate riding school buses for any reason, they always make me feel nauseous, but this trip was a total waste for four more reasons. Reason 1: Unlike Thomas Jefferson, my history teacher wasn't alive in the 1700s and doesn't know jack shit about what happened back then. Reason 2: My teacher never even studied history at university, he was an English major, so I think he makes half this shit up. Reason 3: My teacher is a lazy bastard who probably hasn't read a book since he graduated from teacher's college, which makes me even more certain he makes this shit up. Reason 4: I did my own research the night before, and so I know for a fact the teacher makes shit up. So there was no way I was going to pay attention to anything on that field trip. As soon as we got off the school bus my buddy Aadel and I ditched the rest of the group and went behind the blacksmith's shed, where we sat in the sun and downed some beers we'd hidden in our lunch bags.

For the record, here's what the teacher didn't tell us about the Founding Fathers of Not-Sedro-Woolley: They were a bunch of drunken losers. They couldn't cut it in the places they came from, and settled here because they weren't welcome anywhere else. They scratched out a living by selling homemade whisky to passing travellers, and drank a lot of it themselves. Some tried their hands at farming but they weren't very good at it. Families were big, and the men treated their wives and kids like shit. The smart kids got the hell out. The stupid ones stayed behind, and did much the same thing as their parents did. That's how it went, a bunch of drunken losers passing along derelict houses and ramshackle businesses from one generation to the next until they won the lottery, sort of, in the 1950s. That's when the government built a four-lane highway that by chance happened to pass through this backwater. Developers showed up wanting to build donut shops and cheap motels and strip malls and new subdivision homes alongside the highway. And so the descendants of the first white settlers were able to sell their land for an unexpectedly good price and retire to Florida. Before leaving they named the new streets and schools and stuff after their ancestors. Some of the longest-established losers were from a family named Arthur, so we've got an Arthur Avenue and an Arthur School and an Arthur Park. There are still a few of the original Arthurs around town, most of them stoners.

If you look closely, you'll find that history usually works that way. I bet it's like that in your hometown, too. Take a look at the street names you pass by each day, and ask yourself where they came from. Your town may not have a single street or school named after Teddy Roosevelt, who ought to have something named after him in every town on the planet, but I bet your town has a bunch of streets named after long-forgotten mayors and dead businessmen who were real dicks and did nothing important whatsoever. There's no danger of anyone naming a park or a street after me.

And there's no danger of me or anyone else from Not-Sedro-Woolley getting their face chiseled on a mountain one day. This town doesn't exactly churn out Teddy Roosevelts, if you know what I mean. In two centuries we haven't even churned out a single astronaut, inventor, professional athlete or other noteworthy person. We haven't even had a famous criminal or an internet video sensation. Our most famous citizen is a guy named Brent, who was on CNN before YouTube was invented. Brent had gone off to college but flunked out in the first semester, so he had to move back into his parents' basement. The only time he left the couch was to score some weed or to hit golf balls at the driving range (golf being the ultimate in loser sports). One day Brent was high at the driving range and thought it would be funny to go for a joy ride on the modified lawnmower contraption they use to gather up golf balls. So he took off down the highway on that thing and the owners of the driving range called the cops. Brent led them on a slow-speed chase for the next forty minutes. It was pretty funny. A TV news channel sent a chopper up to film the whole thing, and you realize when you see them from the air that riding lawnmowers don't move very fast. The cops tried to blockade the road but Brent just drove onto the median and went around them. The whole thing ended when he turned off the highway at the next exit, rammed the mower through the front window of a Domino's and tried to gobble as many pizza slices as possible before the cops tackled him. He spent a couple nights in jail and then had to start attending AA for junkies as part of his probation. The Domino's owner gave Brent a job, thinking he could attract more customers if people could order their slices from the same guy who trashed the place on national TV. But no extra customers came, and after four days Brent got caught stealing a ten-pound bag of pepperonis, and was fired.

So there you have it. After two hundred years, the most interesting thing our town ever produced is Brent. It won't surprise you that no TV producers ever asked to make a reality show starring Brent. If they did, it would have to be shown on HBO late at night, since each episode would conclude with Brent jacking off in his parents' basement. And I somehow don't think kids a hundred years from now will be touring his house or memorizing his name for history tests, but maybe he'll get a street named after him. My classmates who want to be famous don't have a very high threshold to cross if they want to become the most notorious person in Not-Sedro-Woolley. All they have to do is accomplish something more interesting than ramming a mower into a pizza joint.

God, I can't wait to get the fuck out of this place.

## Chapter 2: A basket of crabs

The last sentence in the previous chapter isn't exactly true. I can wait a little longer before I leave this place. I don't especially like school, my teachers are far from inspiring, and I don't fit in too well with other kids my age. But even though I'm old enough to quit school, I'm not an idiot. When I say that I can't wait to head west to the real Sedro-Woolley, I'm 100% serious, but I don't want to show up there as a penniless high school dropout. That would defeat the purpose of my plan. For a couple more years I'll keep my head down and my mouth shut, and play along with the whole education thing. When I finish high school after next year I'll go to college and learn a useful skill so I can support myself without any help from anyone. That way when I get out west I'll be able to get a decent job and stay there for good.

If you're like most people who meet me for the first time, you're probably wondering about my name, Landon Go. It is a bit unusual, I will admit. My friends don't bother calling me Landon, they usually just riff off my last name and call me "Go-Pro" or "Go-fer" or stuff like that. Sometimes in the hall one of the stoners will say, "Hey, Go-fuck-yourself" and laugh, but fortunately that doesn't happen too often. My family name is 'Go' because my great-grandfather on my father's side was from Singapore and dropped the h from Goh when he came to this country as a teenager looking for work. Actually, he's my step-great-grandfather. He married a widow woman from Poland and adopted her son (my grandfather) as his own. So if you're trying to picture what I look like, I don't look like I'm from Singapore, even though my name is from there. I've got light brown hair and blue eyes. My Mom called me Landon because when she was young she was obsessed with a TV show called "Little House on the Prairie", and the guy who played the dad on the show was an actor named Michael Landon. Thank goodness her favorite show wasn't Scooby-Doo, I might have been named Fred or Shaggy.

I like to skateboard (and longboard) and I like to read. I probably read more than any other person I know, except for maybe the head librarian at the public library. Who, by the way, is pretty hot even though she's as old as my mom and dresses like she's even older. I mentioned this once to my friends when we were skateboarding past the library and my friend Jeremy looked at me like I was an alien and said, "Are you kidding? She's a barracuda." I'm not sure what he meant, but it was clearly not a compliment. He was probably thinking about some other woman who works in the library, since Jeremy only ever goes in there when he's downtown and needs to take a shit. If he needs to piss he doesn't bother going inside, he just does it behind the supermarket dumpster. We all do.

You might think it's unusual that a skateboarder like me likes to read so much. Skateboarders have a reputation for being empty-headed slackers. True, some of them are (like Jeremy), but not all. And not me. The idea that if you're a skateboarder you must also be a stoner is a nasty stereotype. I don't believe in stereotypes, and you shouldn't either. There's no reason why I can't skateboard and do something really brainiac as well, like compose an opera. Not that I like opera music or have ever been to an opera, but you know what I mean. We're all capable of being many things at the same time.

I like skateboarding for the same reason I like reading: both give me a break from living with six other people. With two parents, two younger brothers, and two younger sisters, our house is always pretty noisy. So I often lock myself in my room with a book or ride my longboard to the outskirts of town to get a little peace and quiet.

I first started reading when I was three. My parents bought an encyclopedia called *The World Book* from a telemarketer. They thought I might use it to do my homework when I got older, but I had read most of the articles in it by the time I hit the first grade. And that's a lot of articles, because that encyclopedia has twenty-one volumes, and each one has at least a couple hundred pages. I was always toting one around the house. If I had to go to the toilet to do a number two, I'd take a volume of *The World Book* with me. Don't ask me why I started reading it or if I even understood it at first, it happened so long ago I don't remember. But by the time I started school I could read all kinds of stuff while the other kids were still learning to recognize the spelling of their own names. In first grade I was sent to the third grade class during reading period, because the first grade stuff was too easy for me. The third graders were reading a series of books about a shaggy sheepdog called Mr. Mugs. I was intimidated being in a classroom with all those older kids, so I kept quiet and just did my work. I was too scared to tell the teacher that Mr. Mugs was way too easy for me.

I moved on from encyclopedias to Hardy Boy mysteries, which my grandmother used to buy me before she died of lung cancer. She smoked like a chimney. I don't smoke at all, it's expensive and smelly and *will* kill you. Hardy Boys were written more than fifty years ago, and the descriptions of teenage life back then are pretty trippy. If you haven't read them, Frank and Joe Hardy are brothers who live in a fictional seaside town called Bayport. Their parents must have had money, because the Hardy Boys have a motorboat and good-looking girlfriends and travel to exotic places like Mexico. Mexico would be cool. Their friends have goofy names like Biff and Chet, and one of them drives a jalopy, which I had to look up in the dictionary. It means a beater car. The Hardy Boys solve mysteries. Some of the mysteries are really interesting, others aren't. Although the Hardy Boy books all say on the cover they were written by Franklin W. Dixon, there is no such person. The publishing company hired a whole bunch of authors to write the books and told them all they had to use the same fake name. I wonder how the authors felt, putting all that time and effort into creating something cool while some imaginary guy named Franklin got all the credit. I hope they got paid well.

They probably didn't. Good artists usually don't get paid well. Same thing with good skateboarders. That's probably why many people who could be awesome writers or skateboarders eventually give up and become accountants or technical sales experts, or just drop out and become full-time stoners. Our society is totally whacked. It values all the wrong things. Humans have evolved these enormous brains that are capable of designing spaceships and finding vaccines to stop killer viruses and writing poetry and growing the most amazing organic fruits and vegetables and carving the most amazing turns on a downhill run. But who gets paid the most money? Bankers and lawyers and stockbrokers and that sort of thing. Think about that for a moment. The most boring and uncreative people in society get paid most. The school principal gets paid more than the teachers. Does that make any sense? I mean, sure, some creative people get paid, like some musicians and one or two painters and some X-Games athletes. But for every super-creative person like Neil Young who gets rewarded properly for his talent there are thousands of wicked musicians who never make any money and end up waiting tables the rest of their lives. I mean, have you heard of Rebox Invariant? I didn't think so. They were an amazing Not-Sedro-Woolley band that could fuse Michael Jackson and Nirvana into one song. Seriously. But they could never get a recording deal, so the lead guitarist ended up taking a job as a firefighter, which meant the band had to split up because he was always working night shifts.

I'm not sure if I qualify as creative person just yet, but I want to be one. I'm not sure exactly what I'll study at college or do for my career, I hope it's not accounting or something like that. I *do* know that I don't want to get all the way to Washington state and have to work a job where you serve fries all day. I mean, that kind of job is fine when you're sixteen, but you sure don't want to be doing it the rest of your life.

My dad wants me to become a software engineer, even though he barely knows how to use a computer and I'm always having to reset his printer or update his anti-virus software for him. My heart sinks whenever I hear him calling from his office,

"Landon, can you come here for a minute?"

which usually means something like he can't find a document file because he stored it in the wrong directory. It would be nice if he actually tried to learn how to operate a computer properly.

The main reason Dad wants me to become a software engineer is because he knew a guy in high school who was into personal computers when they were still new and had less memory than a watch does today. My dad's friend moved west and got a job with Microsoft designing spreadsheet software – an idea they copied from another company called Lotus 1-2-3 – and became a millionaire. So my dad figures if I become a software engineer I'll be a millionaire, too. He doesn't realize there's tons of software engineers in the world now, and a lot of them live in places like India and China where they only get paid a few dollars a day. Besides, I'm not all that interested in writing computer code. I mean, I know how to do it, it's not that hard, but it's boring. So are video games. When I was six years old I liked gaming, but I grew out of it pretty quickly. Most of my friends are gaming when they're not skateboarding. I play a few games with them once in a while just to keep them happy, but I think games are a waste of time. You don't learn anything useful from them, and they just distract you from more important things. There's only twenty-four hours in a day, and if you subtract eight for school and another eight for sleeping and a couple more for eating and doing homework and chores, that doesn't leave much time in the day. I'm certainly not going to waste it gaming.

Because I don't always do what everyone else does, I sometimes stand out as being different. That can be a dangerous thing in high school. Actually, it starts to become dangerous in about the sixth grade. There are people out there who make it their mission in life to put 'different' people in their place. I read once that fishermen don't need to put a lid on a basket of crabs, because if any crab tries to get out the other crabs grab him and pull him back in. I don't know if that is true or not, since I don't live near the ocean, but living in Not-Sedro-Woolley is a lot like living in a basket of crabs. If you start to stand out from the others, they'll try to pull you back down.

For example, there's this guy at our school who calls himself Hashman, because he smokes a lost of hash. Or so he says. He's so full of shit and so incredibly stupid, it's hard to believe anything he says. He lives in the government-subsidized housing estate where a lot of tough guys live, and so he think that makes him tough by association. But I don't think the other tough guys like him. Maybe he has to act tough to survive in that estate. Anyhow, when I started ninth grade I didn't know who he was, though I had heard there was some guy who called himself Hashman. On the first day of school my friend Todd was talking in the hallway to some other guy from our math class. I wandered over and joined the conversation late, and missed the first part of what they'd been talking about. Todd was saying something about Hashman throwing a party at his house and, without thinking, I said something like,

"Why would anyone call himself Hashman? Sounds lame."

Well, it turns out the guy Todd was talking to *was* the Hashman, and he wasn't happy. I was thinking, oh great, now he'll want to fight. But know what he did instead? For the rest of the entire school year he simply pretended that I don't exist. Then, on the very last day of school, he wore a white t-shirt and went through the class asking people to sign it with a marker. When he got in front of my desk he said real loud,

"Not you, Go-fuck-yourself-you-fucking-loser",

and moved on to the next person, making sure everyone could see he had shunned me. Like I care. The clown didn't remember a single thing we learned in math that year, but he remembered to put me in my place when he got the chance. You see what I mean about a basket of crabs?

## Chapter 3: The Leah Effect

OK, I've talked enough about me, time to talk about Leah now. She's the reason why I decided to write this story down in the first place.

Remember how I told you about Brent-the-mower-thief? Well, Brent has a younger sister, Leah, who's really sweet. She was one of the first older girls I noticed when I started high school. I remember it clear as day. We passed each other during class change and she didn't notice me at all because she was talking to a friend. I still don't know exactly what came over me, but the instant I caught that first glimpse of her face, I just totally fell for her. Do you know what I mean? It was like the lyrics from the type of pop songs boy-bands sing for twelve-year-old girls. Pretty sad, I know.

For all of the ninth grade and most of the tenth grade, I kept my crush on Leah to myself. I never had the courage to speak to her. I don't think that's too unusual; what ninth grade boy hasn't been completely awestruck by a hot older girl? Since you don't know her, here's three important things you *should* about her:

(1) Her brother's a loser (you actually knew that already);

(2) She's two years older than me;

(3) She worked a lot of shifts at McDonald's (she still does), mainly at the cash register, where she has to wear an ugly black polyester uniform.

Point 3 presents a bit of a problem in terms of opportunities to encounter Leah outside of school, because I don't go to McD's a lot. I prefer to eat organic food and hang out in independently-owned coffee shops (there are three in Not-Sedro-Woolley), but there was this one Saturday last year when I ended up going to McD's twice, and it was then I had my first close encounter with Leah.

The first time I entered the McD's that day was for an early supper with my parents and all my brothers and sisters. I only went along to keep the peace with my dad. He works crazy long hours as a technical salesman for a Brazilian company. It wasn't always a Brazilian company, and my dad's never been to Brazil (although that would be cool, especially to visit the Amazon rain forest). It used to be a local company that manufactured parts for automobiles. When the owner retired he sold it to some people he thought were Americans, but who turned out to be fronts for a multinational corporation owned by a Brazilian billionaire whose great-grandparents got rich in the 1800s because they owned a sugar plantation and a lot of slaves. I had to do some research to find this stuff out.

I know what you're thinking: since when did Brazilians get so rich that they can buy up our country? Aren't they supposed to be a developing nation? It just goes to show you we aren't as smart or rich or powerful as our politicians and media want us to think.

By the way, Thomas Jefferson also owned slaves and a plantation, so when he wrote in the Declaration of Independence that "All men are created equal" he didn't actually mean it the way he wrote it.

Anyhow, as soon as the Brazilian-owned corporation bought the factory here in Not-Sedro-Woolley, they laid off most of the workers and moved all the machinery down to Mexico, where they pay workers ten percent of what people here were getting. Now there's nothing left in the building but an office for the few sales people they let keep their jobs. They kept my dad because he's a really good salesman. He doesn't talk about it, but I don't think he's very proud to still be working for this company, because a lot of his former co-workers were also his friends and many of them haven't found new jobs yet. The weird thing is, my dad now makes *more* money than he used to. He sells more auto parts than ever before because they don't cost as much since they started manufacturing them in Mexico. I know it's wrong that my family is getting richer because other people got poorer, but I haven't yet figured out what I can do about it. How do you fight the capitalist system when you're just a high school student? It's pretty feeble, but my main way of taking action has been to buy my daily latte only from locally owned coffee shops, and never from the big corporate chains. If I'm going to spend money on coffee, which is my main regular expenditure, I want as much of that money as possible to stay in my community.

By the way, here's an insider tip from a regular latte drinker: ask for non-fat milk, it won't leave a greasy feel in your mouth.

Getting back to my father, after working crazy hours at his job he comes home and goes straight to work in his flower gardens. I would prefer that he grew vegetables because, like the agrarian philosopher Wendell Berry, I think growing your own food is a good way to resist the industrial food complex that laces everything we eat with pesticides and growth hormones and tries to make us all fat and diabetic. But Dad sticks to growing flowers. Which is still OK, because flowers create much-needed habitat for bees and butterflies that are rapidly going extinct. He doesn't garden to save pollinators or as a statement against agricultural capitalism, he says gardening helps him relieve his stress. I'm not sure whether it's his job that's so stressful or if it's having so many kids. Probably both. Anyhow, once every couple weeks or so he will be weeding his garden when he suddenly stops, realizes he's been ignoring the rest of us a lot lately, and announces,

"It's time we all did something together as a family."

I dread those moments. Anything can happen, and it's usually something that either bores or embarrasses me. Like all of us going mini-golfing, or embarking on a 'treasure hunt' at an antique store. One time he actually made us all go curling. Curling! Do you even know what that is? Imagine a bunch of senior citizens in a freezing cold arena, pushing rocks with handles, and madly sweeping the ice with brooms. How it was ever invented is beyond me. The guy who gave our family a curling lesson that day boasted how it was an Olympic sport, which did not impress me, because so is walking (that's true, you can look it up). Also, I am firmly anti-Olympics. They're a scam. Cities that host the Olympics spend bucketloads of money that could be better used to build schools and hospitals, and end up horribly in debt for years to come with nothing to show for it but some unused stadiums. Most importantly, curling and walking are Olympic sports but skateboarding is not. Figure that one out.

One day last summer my dad's big idea for a family outing was a 'fast food treat day', so we all loaded ourselves into the Grand Caravan (which gets worse gas mileage than a Hummer, the idiot's vehicle of choice) and off we went to McD's. Leah was working, and she took our order. She was really cool about it. Even though she could easily have ignored me the way many older kids did, she didn't. She didn't say anything directly to me, but she briefly made eye contact with me and gave me a quick, discrete smile, one that my father didn't notice. She could see I was uncomfortable about being out with the whole family somewhere that I might meet kids from school. She seemed to know intuitively that if my dad had caught her smiling at me, he would have started an embarrassing conversation.

Which he would have. My dad has a loud voice and tries to start conversations with everyone he meets, whether they want to talk to him or not. It's the salesman in him. Had he noticed Leah's smile, he would have started chatting her up on my behalf, thinking he was doing me a favor, and said something mortifyingly stupid like, 'My son doesn't have a girlfriend, maybe he could ask you out on a date'. He does stuff like that. But because Leah was so cool, I was able to order my Filet-O-Fish without being embarrassed. The Filet-O-Fish is the most sustainable sandwich on the McDonald's menu, they use wild-caught pollock from Alaskan waters. Unlike cod, pollock numbers are still reasonably good, and pollock can be caught without destroying the seabed by using drag-nets, the way they have to if they're catching sole. And, eating fish creates a much lower carbon footprint than eating beef from cattle raised in feedlots.

Later that same night I was out skateboarding with my friends and we stopped in at McD's. It was their choice, not mine, and though it really goes against my principles to go there twice in the same day, I was quietly hoping that Leah would still be working. She was. She took our order without saying anything about me being there earlier with my parents. Instead, as we walked up to the counter she gave me a bigger smile than she did the first time, and said,

"Hi Landon."

I was pretty shocked that she even knew my name. My friends were impressed. She is older, after all, and cute, while my friends and I are a ragged bunch of teenage skateboarders who look like we just hit puberty (you know, the zits and all). It's not often that I impress them, and I felt pretty stoked the rest of the night.

I got to thinking about Leah a lot after that day. Not in a bad way. It wasn't like I was thinking about her at night and then beating off or anything like that (any females who might be reading this should be aware, if they're not already, that teenage boys masturbate a lot). It's more like I got to thinking things like, why isn't Leah famous? I know this sounds weird, but I bet her life is far more interesting and meaningful than anything you'll see on an MTV reality show. It's got to be more interesting than her mower-stealing brother's life. I mean, in addition to being super nice and cool and able to put nervous geeks like me at ease, and in addition to working late at night at McD's where she must see some weird shit go down, Leah does a lot of other cool stuff, too.

She ran for student council treasurer and won in a landslide. She lives on a small farm on the edge of town and raises rabbits and alpacas and heirloom chickens that she shows at the County Agricultural Fair each fall (her lazy-ass brother, Brent, refuses to help out with the farm). She also volunteers at a home for mentally handicapped teenagers. As you can see, when I mentioned earlier there were three important things you should know about her, I left a lot of important stuff out.

If I could produce a reality TV show, I would have cameras follow Leah around every day. Call me weird if you like, but it would be the only thing that would get me to watch TV again. I gave up TV eighteen months ago, and I'm glad I did. My brain is much clearer now, and I'm starting to see the world for what it really is. I've realized that corporate greed and excess are ruining peoples' lives all over the world, and not just the people who used to work with my father. You don't realize stuff like that when you're vegetating in front of MTV or zoning out on a video game. It also explains why I don't go to McD's unless my family or friends drag me there. I don't want to contribute to corporate evil any more than I have to.

Another thing about my first Leah encounter was that it shook up one-half of my 2-part life philosophy. In case you missed it in chapter one, part one is that west is best. Part two of my philosophy, which you've probably also figured out by now, is that corporations are evil and control most people like drones. But here's the problem: if a corporation employs someone as nice as Leah, can it be truly and completely evil? 100% evil? I'm not sure that it can. Think of when a flower grows in a crack in a parking lot. It makes beautiful an otherwise gray, apocalyptic landscape. Bees find it, and it makes seeds that find other cracks, and over time the flowers come to dominate and the asphalt nightmare falls to ruin.

Leah is a flower in a parking lot of black polyester uniforms. Standing there behind the counter, she sows seeds of kindness even as she passes out plastic trays of grey-animal-flesh sandwiches, oil soaked potato scraps, and caffeine-infused sugar water. That matters. Her presence in polyester – call it the Leah Effect – means the overall evilness quotient of the fast food industry cannot reach 100%. The most it can be is 99.9999% evil (unless she quits, at which point it reverts to being totally evil). So I've concluded that it's OK to visit McD's when Leah is working, because then I would be rewarding and reinforcing good corporate behavior, and maybe McD's will hire more people like her.

It's funny how a smile from a girl can change your outlook on life.

**Chapter 4: Punks**

One time in math class last February the teacher was explaining fractions, and how you should reduce them to the lowest common denominator if you want to compare them. The denominator is the number in the lower part of a fraction, so, for example, in ¾ the denominator is 4. The teacher explained that if you have a fraction like 9/12, you should reduce it and express it as ¾. I raised my hand and asked why, and he replied,

"It's convention."

Which really means he doesn't know the reason. So I asked a follow up question:

"But maybe 9/12 is the logical way to express the fraction on certain occasions. Like, if you had a 12-slice pizza and ate three slices and your friends asked you how much pizza you had left, it would make more sense to say you had 9/12 of a pizza left instead of saying ¾. That way your friends would know it was a twelve slice pizza to begin with."

I don't remember what the teacher said, I think he just ignored me and moved on with the lesson. In the hall after class I got some gentle teasing about being a math brainiac. It was mostly goofy stuff, like,

"Hey Go-nerd, let's hit McDonald's and grab a 4/12 pounder",

and

"Who eats only three slices of pizza, anyhow?"

It was gentle teasing, like I said, and I laughed along, but it's a good example of how nothing goes unnoticed around here. Everyone's always trying to reduce you to the lowest common denominator of intelligence. Which is usually close to zero.

There's a couple kids in math class that I really admire, Tim and Kyle, though I don't talk to them. In middle school they were total geeks, and a lot of people picked on them. I don't know how you become someone who gets picked on, I just try hard to make sure I don't end up being one. I once saw a *National Geographic* video about wolves in Yellowstone Park. There's thousands of elk and deer and bison in the park that all look the same to us humans, but wolves have some hidden sense they use to single out the animals that are weaker than all the others, and those are the ones they hunt down. Kids are like that. If the pack gets the sense that you're weak, they prey upon you mercilessly. Tim even used to get picked on by the girls. I remember very clearly this one day in the eighth grade when one of my friends came running over saying,

"You got to see this. Sarah is going to beat the shit out of Tim!"

Sarah is a short girl with a really loud voice and a nasty temper. I should note that Sarah is a pretty common name and I know four girls named Sarah or Sara, but only one of them is a bully. So we went running over and, sure enough, there's Tim, leaving the school with his little sister, who he has to walk home each day. Sarah the bully was following a few steps behind them, screaming all sorts of nasty shit, and challenging Tim to a fight. What he did to make her angry, I still don't know. But while she was letting him have it, a crowd of other kids started to form behind her. It became a bizarre parade that lasted for four or five blocks. Tim was in the lead, not saying a word and looking only straight ahead. He had a big smile glued on his face and he held his sister's hand and walked at a steady pace. Next came Sarah, screaming louder than a marching band of bagpipe players, followed by ten or twelve of us, a few encouraging her, others (like me) watching in silent fascination, wondering what would happen next.

Nothing did happen next. Sarah got tired of screaming, and stormed off. Everyone else went their own ways. I stood for a long time watching Tim and his little sister walking into the distance. They looked so noble. I felt so very, very bad for the two of them. They must have been so scared, and I bet they were afraid to go back to school the next day. When I was lying in my bed that night, I started to feel ashamed of myself, for having been one of those kids in the crowd who just followed along and watched. But of course, I've never told anyone that. And though I should have apologized to Tim, I didn't. He probably would have thought I was being weird, anyway.

As it turned out, Tim didn't need my pity. He came back to school the next day and every day after, and mostly just ignored the lot of us. He made a couple really close friends, like Kyle. They were sort of on the margins of the crowd, if you know what I mean. They stuck together through the remainder of eighth grade, and when they were freshmen in high school some girls and a couple other guys joined their group. They continued to keep to themselves, didn't talk much in class, and you didn't see them much outside of school. Then, in the summer after ninth grade, they started listening to classic cool punk music from the UK like the Clash and the Sex Pistols, and even some old Who albums like *Quadrophenia*. The kind of stuff Kurt Cobain listened to. When they came back to school for sophomore year they were all wearing army surplus clothing and Doc Martens, had piercings all over, and Kyle and one of the girls got spiked Mohawks with rainbow colored dye in their hair. For about a week it was all anyone could talk about, but now that some time has passed, I don't think many people give them too much thought.

Tim and his friends don't cause any trouble. They don't act like punks, they're not now a gang or anything. They still get good grades and are respectful to teachers. They just look different. I think it's totally cool and I'm kind of envious. I couldn't dress or look like that myself, because it sends a sort of 'I-don't-give-a-shit' message to the rest of the world, and I am more of a 'I-give-a-shit' kind of person. Maybe you're thinking, what if they go all Columbine and bring guns to school and blow up the place to retaliate against all the kids who used to pick on them. I kind of doubt that would happen. I mean, if Tim was going to do something like that, he would have done it the day after Sarah the bully went after him and the rest of us did nothing to stop it. To be honest, I wouldn't have entirely blamed him if he did, but for obvious reasons I'm pretty glad that he didn't. The fact is, Tim and Kyle and their friends are harmless. Just the same, I bet adults who see them walking down the street cross to the other side just to be safe. And I bet the security guards at the mall hassle them more than they do other kids, although I don't hang out often enough at the mall to have seen it myself. In my experience, most adults fear teenagers who intentionally look different from the others.

There are teenagers around here you really ought to be afraid of, but they aren't the ones who dress like punks. One of the biggest idiots you need to steer clear of is Bennie Dock. Bennie's an athletic looking guy who wears preppy clothes and has a lot of money to throw around. He even got a Hummer when he turned sixteen. His dad owns a couple donut stores and is almost as big an asshole as Bennie. Bennie's mom left the two of them when he was fourteen, and Bennie's dad's girlfriend moved in with them soon after. She has a son named Boz who is eighteen, quit school two years ago, and is very tough. I'm pretty sure he deals meth. Boz hates Bennie's guts, and Bennie is absolutely terrified of him, but Bennie tries to pretend to everyone else that he and Boz are cool and in a gang together. Bennie is a complete and utter loser, and probably the stupidest person on the planet. But because he is athletic and has lots of money and Boz influencing him, Bennie's always trying to prove he's a big-shot bad-ass. He'll be walking down the street and if he thinks no one's looking he will smash in the side window of a parked car and lift anything he can find, even if it's only a few quarters and packs of gum sitting in the console. He'll go to the mall and shoplift stuff he doesn't need, just so he can boast about it at school.

He also likes to rape eighth grade girls. Why eighth grade girls? Because they're easily impressed by high school guys with cars, and are at that age where they're starting to get interested in sex. If you haven't met him before, Bennie can be quite charming in a fake and plastic sort of way, and inexperienced girls easily fall for it. So he's always hanging out in places where the eighth graders hang out, like McD's and stuff. He makes friends with them and invites them over to his house where he's got his expensive sound system and a beer fridge. He always makes sure there's a bunch of them, boys and girls, so that no one suspects what he's really up to. He gets them all partying and if one of the girls is drinking (not all the girls drink, but all the boys do), Bennie starts chatting her up. If she's not getting drunk fast enough or not falling for him, he slips something into her drink when she's not looking. He persuades her to go to his bedroom with him and... you can guess what happens next. He knows that he'll never get into any trouble. The girl is too scared to tell anyone what happened, and if any of her friends saw what happened, they're too scared to say anything because they would have to explain to their parents how they were all getting drunk. And once he's had his fun, Bennie immediately turns into a mean and intimidating shit, and threatens the kids to keep their mouths shut, or else. Worst thing is, I hear Bennie's got a nasty case of herpes.

Bennie has a serious hate on for me, even though I've barely ever spoken to him and hardly know him. I think it's because of this. One time about a year and a half ago Bennie decided he wanted to be a skateboarder, so he went out and dropped $500 on a beautiful board none of the rest of us could ever afford and came to the park to hang with me and my friends. None of us is exactly Tony Hawk, but Bennie was awful. He could barely stand up on it. At first we kind of joked about it and he was laughing too, although I don't think he thought it was funny, and we made sure we didn't laugh too hard in case he wigged out. But after a while, it stopped being funny at all and just got sad. Everyone started to get really quiet. After trying to do an Ollie for about the fiftieth time, Bennie wilsoned hard on his ass and hurt his tailbone. The others pretended not to see, but I couldn't help it, just for a split second I looked at him and we made eye contact. I could see the embarrassment and shame in his eyes and how he was trying hard not to cry. I looked away really fast, but he realized that I saw him for what he really is, a pathetic little chickenshit. I never said a word about it to anyone, but from that day on, he has hated me. He just glares at me whenever I'm in his vicinity. I know that if I were ever unlucky enough to bump into him somewhere alone, he would try to lay a beating on me, or worse. So I make sure that never happens.

My point is this: it's true when people say you shouldn't always judge a book by its cover. Bennie looks like a Mr All-American preppy guy who might become President one day, but he's a sick puppy. Tim and Kyle look like freaks, but they'd probably turn out to be really nice guys if you got to know them. They've certainly got their friends' backs.

As for me, I'm a book still in search of its cover.

## Chapter 5: Tiina

You're probably wondering how I learned all that creepy stuff about Bennie if I've never hung out with him. Tiina told me. And yes, that's how her name is spelled. She's named after her grandmother, who came from Finland, where Tina is spelled with two i's. Who's Tiina? It goes something like this...

One day two summers ago I was hanging out in my friend Aadel's basement rec room. Another person with a double-vowel name. Aadel's parents immigrated from Afghanistan back in the 1990s, after their country had been turned into a shithole by Russian invaders. Russians are kind of like the Bennies of world politics. When Aadel's parents got here they barcly had two dimes to rub together. They worked any jobs they could find and eventually scraped together enough money to put a down payment on a fleabag motel out by the highway, called the Dutch Motor Inn. You've no doubt seen this type of place. It's one long, low building with all the doors facing out into the parking lot, with a plastic chair, a table, and an ashtray in front of each one. There was a derelict outdoor swimming pool off the parking lot, and the only thing scarier than the rooms was the people who rented them. But Aadel's parents slowly fixed it all up, and it started to make good money. For most of his life Aadel lived with his brother and parents in a small apartment behind the motel office. A few years ago they bought a nice brick house in my neighborhood. Some of our neighbors didn't like it, they worried that other immigrants might also want to move into the neighborhood, and they tried to make his family feel unwelcome. Fortunately my parents aren't hung up on such things. Aadel doesn't get hassled too much by the other kids in the neighborhood or at school, since he was born here and is a pretty big guy. I also think – or at least, I hope – that people my age aren't as hung up on race as older people are. But his parents still experience a lot of racism. You know, really stupid mean stuff, people calling them 'Pakis' and treating them ignorantly in restaurants and shops, telling them to speak English properly (they still have accents). Even though his folks are the sweetest people in the world, work their asses off, and now have more money than many people in Not-Sedro-Woolley, some idiots just have to go out of their way to remind them that they're not from here. I just don't get racism, it makes no sense. If you're a racist, please stop reading this right now. Seriously. I don't want you reading my story. Get your ass to a therapist or counselor or something, because there's something wrong with your head. And if you're not willing to do that, then go fuck yourself.

OK, back to the story. We were in Aadel's basement, listening to some music, not doing a whole lot. Aadel had this sort-of girlfriend, Emma, and she and her friends would sometimes drop in at his place. On that particular day Emma stopped in with her sister, who's a year older than her, and three other girls. Two of the other girls I knew, the third I only vaguely recognized. That was Tiina. Tiina had bumped into the other girls down at the pizza shop, and when she heard they were going to stop in at Aadel's, Tiina asked if she could tag along. She explained to Emma that she was sort of interested in me, and hoped I'd be at Aadel's. Although we had gone to the same middle school, Tiina was a grade behind me. She also lives at the exact opposite end of town from me. Maybe that's the reason I hadn't noticed her before.

I need to learn to pay better attention, because Tiina's pretty cute. She's also pretty forward, which is a good thing for me, because I am very shy and awkward around girls. If it were up to me to make the first move, I would probably never have kissed a girl and maybe never would. So when Tiina showed up with Emma and her friends at Aadel's, she immediately came straight over to where I was on the couch, sat down next to me, and just started talking away like we were old friends. In less than three minutes she made it clear that (1) she had a thing for intelligent guys; (2) she liked me; and (3) she wanted to get to know me better. So we left, walked down to the park, sat on a picnic table, and talked for a couple hours.

I can't tell you everything we talked about, since she did 90% of the talking and I didn't quite follow it all. I was having trouble paying attention, because I was in The Zone, if you know what I mean. It's not every day that you walk out of the house with nothing to do and you end up spending your afternoon with a cute girl who's into you. At least, that certainly doesn't happen to me every day. It was during that long conversation Tiina told me about Bennie, because she wanted to know if I hung out with him and she wanted to see my reaction to what he said he did to eighth grade girls. When I asked her why none of the girls called the cops, she told me I was pretty naïve, but she liked the fact that I asked the question. When I told her about the skateboarding incident and that I thought Bennie wanted to kill me because of it, she was pleased. And when it got close to dinnertime she said she had to go, but asked me if I would meet her back in the park after midnight. Of course I said yes, though I knew it wouldn't be just the two of us.

I don't know how it got started, but that summer a lot of people I knew had started sneaking out of their homes in the middle of the night, after their parents were asleep, to go hang out at the park until four in the morning when they'd sneak back into the house. They only did this on weeknights, when their parents had to go to work in the morning. It's surprisingly easy to do this without getting caught. Working parents with teenaged kids tend to be pretty exhausted and sleep-deprived, so once their heads hit the pillow they don't budge until the alarm goes off. You could drop a stack of dishes in my parents' bedroom at midnight and not wake them.

Most of my friends had been doing this for several weeks, but until Tiina came along I hadn't bothered. I like my sleep. My friends said it was all pretty cool, nobody went crazy or anything when they were down there at the park at night. They knew that if they made a ton of noise or got out of hand, some neighbor would call the cops and it would all quickly come to an end. Some nights they'd build a small campfire, but most times they didn't. Some nights they'd have a couple beers with them or a small bottle of Southern Comfort that someone swiped from their parent's liquor cabinet, which would be mixed with so much Coke to make it go around that no one got more than a gentle buzz. Don't ask me why it was almost always Southern Comfort. My guess is that it's the kind of booze parents open at Christmas when they're entertaining guests and they forget about it for the rest of the year. My friend Todd, whose older brother is a dealer, would sometimes show up with a big Bob Marley spliff. But mostly, everyone just kind of hung out and talked and laughed. Some nights it was just guys there, but most of the time there were as many girls as guys.

When I got down to the park at about 12:30, Aadel and four or five of my other friends were already there. Tiina was there, too, along with Emma and some other girls. In fact, the numbers were equal, guys to girls, once I arrived. Unfortunately, a few minutes later Bennie arrived, riding a brand new BMX bike he got that day. I tried not to groan. He tried not to notice me. Bennie opened his backpack and pulled out a big bottle of Southern Comfort and a deck of cards. He proposed that everyone should take a drink straight from the bottle, and then he would deal out the cards in a certain way so that each of the guys would be randomly paired up with one of the girls. The idea was that each pair would then go off alone together to talk or hang out or make out or whatever for a while. With his arrival, there was suddenly one more guy than girls, and you could tell from his attitude that I was going to be the one left out. But before he could get started, Tiina told Bennie to take the first drink (she didn't trust him and his booze, for obvious reasons). Once he did, she grabbed the bottle from him, took a big slug, handed it back to him and said,

"We don't want to play your silly card game."

She grabbed my hand and led me away from the group. I could feel Bennie's eyes burning a laser hole through my back, and I was thinking, now he's going to kill me for sure the first chance he gets, but I couldn't care less.

Tiina led me over to a big maple tree beside a soccer field. I sat down with my back to the tree, and started thinking about what to talk about, but she wasn't interested in talking. She sat down on top of me and started to kiss me. She was the second girl I had really kissed – you know, with tongues and all – to that point in my life. There have been two others since then, if you're keeping score. The first I ever kissed was Melissa, my eighth-grade girlfriend. Melissa played on the girls' varsity basketball team and I played on the boys' varsity team. She looked pretty good in her basketball uniform, and I sure looked like a dork in mine. Guys as skinny as me shouldn't have their arms hanging out of a sleeveless shirt, and my shoulder-length hair made me look even less athletic, if that's possible. I wear it shorter now, but I don't think anyone's going to mistake me for an athlete.

For whatever reason, Melissa took an interest in me and (thank God once again for forward girls) flirted with me on the bus ride home from an away game in the next town over. We started going out, as much as eighth graders can, and we spent a lot of time practicing our kissing. She was good at it, and I got pretty good at it myself, if you don't mind me bragging a little. But I now realize that one of the reasons we spent so much time kissing was that I was afraid to go any farther. Not because I didn't want to go any farther. I certainly did. It was more like I had a hard time communicating with her, and was never really sure what she wanted. I was afraid that if I tried to go too far too fast, she might get angry and ditch me. The first time I ever touched her on the breasts, she literally had to take my hand and plop it down on one of them. Same with her bum.

I never got any farther with her because she got bored with me moving too slow and started going out with a high school guy named Dick. I'm not making it up, his name really was Dick. I don't think Dick wasted any time making sure their relationship got considerably more physical than mine had been with her. I wasn't heartbroken over losing her, but I hadn't gotten much female attention until Tiina came along.

Back to Tiina and me under the tree. I had learned from my mistake with Melissa, so after Tiina and I had kissed for a while, I moved my hands onto her bum and then into her shirt, which she liked. Then she started to unbutton my jeans and then...

"What's that smell?"

she stopped and said. And sure enough, there was this awful smell in the air that we hadn't noticed until after I had sucked all the Southern Comfort off her tongue. I put my hand down on the ground and realized that I had been sitting in an enormous pile of dog shit. A St. Bernard or a Great Dane must have dropped a fresh load there only a few hours earlier, and I had just spent several minutes grinding those turds into every pore of my Levi's with a hot girl on my lap. Only now she was cooling down rapidly, and I was feeling kind of gross myself.

I went home. I mean, what else could I do? After I told Tiina what I'd been sitting in, she hopped off me, and I stood up. We looked at each other awkwardly, and I said I would call her. And so she nodded and went back to find her friends. I never did end up calling her, because after she went back to the group, she started talking to my friend Dale. Dale's kind of quiet like me and is the most thoughtful of any of the guys I hang out with. Tiina told him what had happened and, unlike most of my other friends, who would have started hooting and telling everyone how I sat in shit like a total loser, Dale simply said that he felt bad for me. This made a favorable impression on Tiina, and they got to talking, and he asked her if he could call her the next day. Which he did, and to cut a long story short, they're still going out together and I wouldn't be surprised if they get married as soon as they're finished high school. So it's a good thing for them that I rolled in dog shit that night. And it's a good thing for me, too, because if I hadn't, I might now be in a committed relationship with Tiina, which would get in the way of my plans to head west for the real Sedro-Woolley. I can't have anyone here tie me down. Although if someone could tie me down, it would be Tiina.

## Chapter 6: Vandenfarts

As it turned out, I didn't have to worry about Bennie killing me. His dad split up with his girlfriend and he left town for the opposite end of the state, taking Bennie with him. Since then I mostly just have to watch out for Vandenfarts. That's not their real name, which is a Dutch one that only sort of sounds like Vandenfart, but since they are such a bunch of assholes I thought I'd modify it to something that sounds more anal. The Vandenfarts are a family with six boys who live a few blocks from me. One of them is a year younger than me, another is a year older, and the rest are older than him. They're a pretty mangy looking bunch, dumb as stumps, with long scraggy hair, who wear mirrored sunglasses and black Nickelback concert t-shirts. (I know. I cringe to even write the word 'Nickelback'). I'm sure you've got plenty of guys like them in your hometown, too. Vandenfarts drop out of school when they're sixteen and spend the rest of their lives trying to avoid getting a job. There's more than one family like that here in Not-Sedro-Woolley, but it's my bad luck that this particular family lives so close to me. I have to pass their house on my way to school and when I do, I pick up my skateboard and walk, because they seem to be attracted to noise.

Vandenfarts are always looking for a fight, even though none of them is very strong and none of them is a good fighter. The one who's three years older than me, Mickey, thinks he knows martial arts because he watches a lot of kung fu movies. If you ever end up fighting him (and I did once, I'll tell you about it in a minute) he starts the fight by running straight at you and launching a sort of flying kick from about five feet away. But he doesn't know what he's doing and it's easy to avoid. The problem with Vandenfarts is that they never, ever, fight one on one. There's always at least two of them when they're looking for trouble. When I was in the seventh grade I delivered newspapers and flyers on Saturday mornings to make a few bucks. One winter morning halfway through my route the two youngest Vandenfarts came shuffling along, mouths flapping. One of them started pushing me, trying to get me to fight. I tried to avoid it as long as I could, but finally the clown took a swing at me, which I dodged. I hit him back, hard enough to make him stop but not hard enough to actually hurt him. If I did hurt him, I would no doubt get jumped by a couple of older Vandenfarts the next day. As I was lightly punching out one Vandenfart, the other one (the smallest Vandenfart) grabbed my bag of newspapers and flyers and started scattering them up and down the sidewalk. The two of them ran off, laughing their guts out, while I gathered up the enormous mess of soggy newsprint. When I got home, my dad asked what happened to my papers, so I explained, and he said,

"Well that's what you get for fighting with other kids."

That attitude is what my Dad calls "tough love". I have a different word for it, starts with 'bull'.

I haven't had too many run-ins with Vandenfarts lately, but in the ninth grade I had a big one right after the first dance of the year. I was pretty stoked that night, I had been looking forward to my first high school dance for a long time. I had heard the girls get all dolled up, and I wasn't disappointed. The older girls looked especially hot. Leah wasn't there, she was working at McD's, as usual. I would have liked to see what she looked like in something other than her black polyester work uniform or the baggy sweats she usually wore to school. Before the dance my buddies and I hung out at the back of the schoolyard and shared a few beers Aadel's brother scored for us. His brother is only eighteen but he's as hairy as a forty-year-old Greek wrestler, so no one ID's him.

Inside the gym it was dark, and they had a decent but not great DJ. I don't know the tradition at your school, but at mine the DJ typically plays a wide range of songs to try to appeal to everyone, with the slow songs being country. I like country music, even though it's not appreciated by most skateboarders. I'm a big fan of Johnny Cash, who must have been a real outlaw. Adults get down on rap music because they say it's all about killing people and getting rich and obsessing about girls, but ask them and they'll all say they like Johnny Cash. But have you heard any of his songs? He's got one where he sings how he killed a man just to watch him die, another where he sings he's going to Jackson town to teach the women there things they don't know. And did you hear the cover he did of that Trent Reznor drug song, 'Hurt'? Very bleak. So next time you hear someone dis on rap music, mention Johnny Cash.

Anyhow, back to the dance. I sat out the first country song, as did all of the younger students. On the dance floor were a few juniors and seniors. All us freshmen sort of split up to either side of the gym, girls on one side, boys on the other, checking each other out. Just as the song was about to end a couple of the braver guys went over and asked girls to dance, and a couple girls did the same. A really good DJ would have noticed this and gone with another country song so more of us would have the chance to brave up and get out there, but this guy went back to playing fast ones. Next up was, 'You Make Me Want to Shout' by Otis Day and The Knights, and all us guys went charging out and started flopping around on the gym floor. If you don't know what I'm talking about, watch the first half hour of the movie *Animal House*. My friends and I love that movie. After that we had some adrenalin flowing through our blood, along with the can and a half of Old Milwaukee each of us chugged in the schoolyard.

When the next country song came up, we all got braver. I decided to ask a girl named Mara to dance. I didn't know her well, even though she was in my grade. She lived in the government subsidized housing, a part of town I don't spent much time in. We danced, twirling in a slow circle to a Dixie Chicks song. She didn't say much, and I'm not a great talker either, especially when I'm nervous (which I was). She was wearing a really nice sweater that was maybe a little thick for the gym and made her unusually warm to the touch.

When the song was over she went over to rejoin her friends. I stopped to talk to Aadel. A few moments later there was some sort of disturbance at the other side of the gym and the music paused. I left the gym to use the washroom, and was standing at the urinal when the third-oldest Vandenfart (the flying kicker) came in and started pissing in the urinal right beside me. You know that's bad news, because men's washroom etiquette is that if all the urinals are vacant, you pick one at the very end. The next guy picks one at the opposite end. You only pick the urinal immediately next to someone else if there's no other option. I know I don't need to explain this to other guys, but if there's any ladies reading this, now you know why I started to tense up. Sure enough, the Vandenfart says to me,

"You're dead."

Needless to say, I desired some clarification as to why I was about to meet my mortal end.

"May I ask why?"

"You made a mistake asking Mara to dance. She's my best friend's girlfriend, and he's pissed."

"Whose girlfriend?"

I couldn't think of who that might be. Vandenfarts don't really have best friends, although they do have some shabby types that hang around them.

"Eddie Murphy's. Eddie wants you to meet him out on the football field after the dance, so he can kill you. You'd better be there."

With that he zipped up and left (without washing his hands, of course).

Now don't be confused, but there really is a guy at our school called Eddie Murphy. He looks nothing like the comedian who's the voice of the donkey in Shrek, although he *does* look like a donkey. Not-Sedro-Woolley's Eddie Murphy is without a doubt, the stupidest person I have ever met, even stupider than that Bennie turd I told you about. Eddie's a tall skinny guy white guy with wild blond hair and a Nickelback t-shirt (where do you even buy those things?) who lives near Mara. I knew that no girl would pay any attention to Eddie unless she was blind and deaf, and Mara was neither. But I guess Eddie somehow got it into his head that Mara was sweet on him, and so he was pissed off when I was the first person to dance with her. I also found out later he had been on his way across the gym to pick a fight with me but he tripped over his own feet, fell hard on the gym floor, puked up the gallon of Hawaiian Punch and rum he'd chugged before the dance, and was immediately chucked outside through the fire door by the phys-ed teacher. That was the disturbance that had stopped the music, and explains why Vandenfart had to act as Eddie's message boy.

I wasn't much afraid of Eddie Murphy. One time I was downtown at the library flipping through a *National Geographic* in a chair near the main door. Suddenly the front door opened wide and there stood Eddie with a lit firecracker in his hand shouting,

"Say your prayers you bunch of losers!"

I think he intended to chuck the firecracker into the library and watch everyone's reaction when it exploded. Only he must have lit the firecracker too early, because it went off in his hand. He started howling in pain, clutching his hand. The hot librarian I mentioned earlier came dashing over and led him to the family washroom so he could run cold water over his burnt hand. So I wasn't too worried about him "killing" me, notwithstanding Mickey Vandenfart's warning. I figured that if Eddie wanted to challenge me to a fight after the dance, it was probably best that I show up, otherwise word might get around that I was afraid of him, and then every weirdo at school would be challenging me.

I went back into the gym and told some of my friends about it, and they said they'd come along to back me up. By the end of the dance I wasn't feeling quite so brave, though. The rumor had spread that there was going to be a big time brawl out on the field, and I could already see dozens of guys leaving for it. Gulp. Rather than walk straight from the gym to the field, my friends and I went out a secondary door and kind of looped around the outside of the school property, so we could come up on the field from the opposite direction from which we were expected. There must have been at least thirty guys hanging around, half of them I didn't know. But at least none of them were any bigger than me, and most looked like they were there to watch and not to fight. My friends looked at me to see what I would do.

For the first time in my life, other people were looking at me to be a leader. But I had no time to make any kind of decision, because almost immediately I heard someone yell from the field,

"There they are!"

There was no choice at that point, leaving would mean turning our backs and running, and you do not run. So I started walking calmly toward the crowd that was running toward us, trying to spot Eddie Murphy among them. As you might expect, he was hiding in their midst. At the front was the third-oldest Vandenfart, who headed straight toward me saying,

"So which one of you is looking for a fight?"

as if he wasn't the guy who set this up. As soon as he got close to me, sure enough he launched a flying drop kick. I stepped to one side and he landed on his ass, and I think he might have hurt his tailbone (sound familiar, Bennie, you asswipe?), since he was slow in getting up and was no longer looking to scrap. One of the younger Vandenfarts pushed Eddie Murphy toward me, saying,

"There he is, dude. Go get him."

Now I will confess, I felt scared. Eddie looked even more scared. Neither of us was scared of the other, we were scared of the idiotic situation we had gotten into. With this many teenage guys all jacked up and looking forward to a fight, things can easily get out of control and something really bad can happen.

Eddie said in a brave voice,

"You shouldn't hit on my girl like that, loser."

"I know she's not your girl."

Now Eddie had no choice, I had called him out, so he had to take a swing at me. Which he did and, even though I thought I saw it coming, he managed to clip me over the right eye with his fist while I was trying to dodge it. Maybe the Old Milwaukees had impaired me more than I thought. My eyebrow burst open and started gushing blood. I stepped forward and hit Eddie square on his nose, which also started gushing blood. For good measure I pushed him onto the ground. Now, this is the point when things can get dangerous. When one of the fighters is on the ground, the spectators want to see more blood. I could sense they wanted me to put the boots to him, but there's no way I'm ever going to kick another person when they're down. So I just leaned over him and said,

"You steer clear of me from now on, Eddie",

and walked away. The younger Vandenfart followed me halfway across the soccer field, taunting and daring me to go back to the fight. But as soon as he realized we were far enough away from the rest of the crowd that no one could help him if I turned and came after him, he retreated, calling me a chickenshit as he scampered away.

I woke up the next morning, a Saturday, with a nice lumpy bruise over my eye. I had managed to slip into the house the night before without my parents seeing me. When I came down for breakfast one of my brothers said,

"Whoa-what-happened-to-you?"

My dad looked at me and was surprisingly calm. He said,

"Looks like you had a fight last night. How does the other guy look?"

"Probably about the same."

"Well, that's a good outcome, I think."

and no more was said about it. By the time Monday came around, most people at school had forgotten about the fight. My friends told me that after I left the fight no one knew what to do, so they all just went home. I haven't had any serious problems with Vandenfarts since then, except for being occasionally called a "fag" when one of the younger ones passes me in the school hallway or on the street. Things could be far worse.

## Chapter 7: Eve

Being called a "fag" is a pretty typical insult among teenage boys. I've probably used it myself, although I know it's wrong, and I generally try not to insult other people anyhow. I've never met an openly gay guy before, although there's a couple guys around school that I get the feeling might be gay or might start dating other guys once they graduate. There's a senior girl who everyone says is a lesbian, and she does nothing to dispel the rumors. I bring this stuff up now because of something that happened in English class this past year.

Each year our school has a day where everyone is told that it's ok to be gay or trans-gendered. The school board prints up a bunch of posters that get hung in the hallways, and in the morning announcements students are told they can come to the guidance office that day to meet confidentially with a special counselor to discuss their sexuality. Of course, no one ever does. I mean, there is no way you could ever get in and out of the guidance office on Gay Day without someone noticing you, and then your need to talk confidentially about your sexuality would be the main topic of conversation in the cafeteria the next day. A couple parents make their kids stay home from school on Gay Day because their religion forbids homosexuality and they don't believe it should be taught in schools. One of the kids who has to stay home on Gay Day is a guy in my grade named Brandon. His mother walked out on his dad three years ago after his dad was caught screwing another woman in the back of the family's minivan while it was parked in the church parking lot.

The woman he was screwing is now Brandon's step-mom, and she is the mother of another kid at our school, a freshman girl named Chastity. For over a year Chastity's mom had been telling Chastity's real dad that she was going to church choir rehearsal when in fact she had been surfing the back seat on Brandon's dad. So now Bandon and Chastity and their brothers and sisters all live together with their new parents in a big farmhouse way out of town, and they have to attend church even more than they used to, probably because their parents feel guilty about their own behavior. All I can say is that Brandon and Chastity both look pretty miserable whenever you see them at school. Stuff like this confirms my skepticism of organized religion. The Ten Commandments in the bible say very clearly you shouldn't covet your neighbor's wife, and I'm pretty sure that boning her in the church parking lot is pretty much the same as coveting her. But apparently God will forgive that sin so long as you don't send your kids to school on Gay Day.

Anyhow, last Gay Day our English teacher asked the class to write a short, reflective passage that expressed our feelings on subject of being gay. I didn't really have any strong feelings, so instead I wrote a short story about a freshman boy who isn't sure whether he's gay or not. He's on the football team. One day when changing after practice he takes too long a look at his naked teammate, who flips out and starts calling him a fag. The kid ends up quitting the football team, starts to get bullied a lot, quits school, and ends up on the street doing drugs, all because his teammate called him a fag, and even though the kid didn't even know if he was gay or not.

The teacher collected all our papers, and then read out extracts from what he thought were some of the more interesting submissions. He promised he wouldn't name whoever wrote them. The first couple he picked were pretty bland, ones where students had regurgitated what was written on the posters in the hall or wrote what they figured the teacher wanted to hear. Then the teacher looked at mine and read my story from start to finish. It took him several minutes to read it, and the class was silent by the end. Then my friend Mitchell, who sits in the next row, looked over at me and said in a loud voice,

"Landon, did you write that?"

So much for my confidentiality, I'd been called out. What could I do? I said yes, and could feel my face getting hot and red. I looked at the teacher for help. What did he do? He simply said that it's a thoughtful piece of writing, and that I have a future as an author.

Word got around the school about my story, and people, especially the guys, started looking at me funny, as if trying to figure out whether I'm gay or not. Fortunately I never played football, otherwise who knows what would have happened in the locker room. A couple of senior girls came up to me during class change, and said,

"We think it's ok if you're gay",

not as a joke, but all serious and sympathetic-like. When I told them I wasn't, they said, oh, that's too bad, a lot of girls thought you were kind of cute and brave for coming out in English class like that. Coming out? Oh, great.

Fortunately Eve came to my rescue. I haven't mentioned Eve previously because she didn't figure into this story until now. She only moved to Not-Sedro-Woolley last year. She sat behind me in English class, and we talked from time to time. We don't have much in common. She is originally from San Francisco, where her dad was a big shot at a high-tech company. I'm not completely sure why her dad moved her here, but he did, just the two of them. Her mom stayed in California. I would have stayed there, too, if I were in her shoes.

They say that California girls are all beautiful. I wouldn't know for sure. Eve is the only girl from California I ever met, and she certainly is beautiful. She's easily the best looking girl at our school, by far. But none of the guys ever hit on her. She made it very clear from the moment she arrived that she was here against her will, and had no intention of making any meaningful connection to any of us or to our town. She dresses differently from everyone else, she is into music and bands that none of us has heard of, she's a vegan, she paints watercolors... you get the picture. Imagine the complete opposite of your average Not-Sedro-Woolley teenager and you've got Eve. Although I've never been to San Francisco, I imagine there's a lot of people like her there, and not many bumpkins like we all are. It was Eve who got me really interested in good quality coffee and organic food and stuff like that. Now that I think about it, she probably had a big influence on both parts of my two-part life philosophy.

Everyone else thinks Eve's a total snob but I don't. As I said, we started having conversations in English class and, although I don't think she has ever considered me a friend, she was friendlier to me than she was to anyone else at school. I would sometimes sit with her at lunch or go for a walk with her around the schoolyard on days 2 and 4 in the school calendar, when we both had the same spare period. I would have spent more time hanging around with her if I could, but she was often off doing her own thing. Our time together happened mainly when she wanted it to.

Eve put an end to the rumors about me being gay after I wrote that story. She told some people around school she knew had big mouths that she had been with me – you know, like *been* with me – and that I certainly wasn't gay. At first I was not sure how I felt about her saying that. I mean, it did stop people gossiping and speculating about my sexuality, although they probably would have stopped anyhow, sooner or later. Instead of being bugged for being maybe gay, I got massively interrogated by my friends, who wanted to know when I started seeing Eve and where we did it and how often and all that. And when I said that I wouldn't mind being with Eve but it hadn't ever actually happened, they just laughed and said,

"Yeah, right Go-Daddy, trying to be cool about it, are you?"

and stuff like that.

The more I got bugged about having sex with Eve, the more I wished she hadn't said we did it. She hadn't asked me how I felt about people thinking I was gay, she simply assumed I couldn't handle it and that she needed to protect me. I'm not sure she realized that I'm like her in many ways, that I really don't care what other people in Not-Sedro-Woolley think of me. I'm different from the yokels around here, but she obviously saw me as being just like them, and that hurt. Eve, of anyone, ought to have realized that I'm different, and happy to be different.

So I sulked. I didn't sit with her at lunch the next day, and I didn't look for her during my spare, even though it was day 4. I didn't talk to her in English class either, I just pretended I was too busy doing my work. After school she was waiting for me out by the tennis courts that I skate past on my way home. I guess I could have ignored her, but I didn't. I skated up to her, stopped my board and looked at her without saying anything.

"What's wrong with you?"

she asked. After hesitating for a moment, I blurted out everything I just wrote two paragraphs above (you know, about how I'm different, just like her). She stared at me for what seemed like ages with her arms folded. God she looked good in her vintage Bruce Springsteen concert t-shirt and cut-off shorts. My guts started to twist inside me. She grabbed my hand and ordered,

"Come on."

She led me past the tennis courts to an overgrown field near the school that's been staked and surveyed for new subdivision homes to be built next year. She sat down in the long grass and sat me down next to her, the outside of our thighs touching. I set my skateboard down on my side opposite her.

She asked,

"How stupid are you? You say you don't need my help, that you can look after yourself, that it doesn't matter what people think of you. Fuck that! You have no idea what you're saying. You have no idea what it's like to be an outsider. No idea. You have your skateboarding friends and your family and all of them like you, even though you kind of drift in and out of their lives whenever you please. You think you don't care what people around here think about you, but you do. You're so insecure – I don't know why, but you are – and you cover it up by acting like you're just putting in time and can't wait to leave them all behind..."

Eve's voice had gotten angry, but after yelling all of this and more things like it at me, she stopped suddenly, and started to sob. This was the first time I'd ever been alone with a crying girl, but I'd seen enough movies to know that the right thing for the guy to do in this situation is to gently put an arm around her. I did, and she grabbed at me and pulled me so tight to her it actually pushed some of the wind out of my lungs. It also gave me an instantaneous, rock-hard erection, which I hid by shifting my hips away from her. Is it wrong that the whole time she was crying, I was enjoying how soft and warm she felt? That I was luxuriating in the sensation of her nipples (which were hard) against my chest? Or how the shuddering of her body against mine sent me into what can only be described as a state of pure tantric Enlightenment, where the rest of the world and all its sentient and non-sentient contents melt away and there is no past and there is no future and there is only light and warmth and the only sounds are your own heart and hers?

After she'd finished crying, she let go of me and lay back. I lay back beside her. She said,

"I hate it here. I wish my father had never brought me here. But I also hate the fact that everyone knows I hate it here, and for that reason I can never be friends with them, even if I wanted to, which I don't. I know that a lot of people around here think I'm a freak and a snob, and I don't care most of the time, but it wears you out being an outsider. Why would you want to be an outsider, Landon?"

I started to launch into my story about wanting to head west as soon as I got the chance, but Eve had heard it before, and interrupted me.

"Stop talking bullshit."

When I swore it wasn't BS, that I really was going to make for Sedro-Woolley after college, she said,

"I believe you when you say you want to head west one day, and you probably will. But you are more a part of this place than you pretend to be. You are loved here, and this will always be where you are from, and you will always carry a bit of this place with you, whether you stay or leave."

She continued,

"That is why I started the rumor that we had been together. That story you wrote about the football player who doesn't know if he's gay was harmless, but the fact that it made the other students question who you are was not harmless. Even in a big city like San Francisco, the gay kids and the suspected gay kids get picked on and isolated at school. In a small-minded place like this it can get a lot worse. I know you know that, and I know you think you could handle it, and maybe you could. But your hate for this town and the people in it would start to become real, it wouldn't be just the pretend-hate you carry with you now. And I thought that would be really sad. So that's why I put an end to all that silliness."

I let her words sink in for a moment or so. She was right, of course. I asked,

"But what about your reputation? Don't you realize people are talking about you now, about – you know – how we had sex and everything?"

Eve laughed, and said she didn't care about that, it isn't like it's the 1950s anymore. She asked me,

"Are you a virgin?"

I squirmed and said,

"What do you mean by a 'virgin'?"

and she laughed again, and said she figured as much. So I told her about my romantic encounters with Melissa and Tiina, which I've already told you about. She asked,

"So why didn't you have sex with either of them? They clearly wanted to have sex with you."

So I told her the truth as best I could. That, as much as I wanted to be having sex with girls – and I really do – it just isn't something I want to rush into. When I have sex with a girl, I want my first time to be totally cool, and not just a bunch of animal-like thrashing and groping in a vacant lot or in a bathroom, trying to get done before we get caught. With a girl who's really nice and who I like to be around, and not someone I get together with at a party where we're both half-wasted and I'd rather forget as soon as it was over.

Eve smiled but didn't laugh, and said,

"You're the first genuinely romantic boy I've ever met. It's nice. But it's too bad you went and made that noble little speech. I lost my virginity at a house party somewhere, half-wasted. And while you were holding me I was thinking I wouldn't mind doing a little groping and thrashing here in this vacant lot. But that would be pretty unromantic, now that I think about it."

With that she kissed me on the cheek, stood up, and left me.

## Chapter 8: The mysterious case of Todd and Summer

For about a week after our encounter in the vacant lot, I walked around moon-eyed for Eve. Had she told me to crawl down the school corridor barking like a dog, I would have done it to please her. But she didn't pay any more or less attention to me than she had before. Things between us were pretty much the same as they had always been, and I began to wonder if I had only imagined what had happened.

Two Saturday nights later I was out with my buddies at a bush party, having a couple Old Milwaukees and trying not to think about Eve, who wasn't there. She didn't usually go to bush parties, but I was quietly hoping she might this time. Do you have these where you live? A bush party is where everyone gets together for a bonfire in a forest or a field, usually on the property of one of the kids who lives out in the country. They can be pretty fun, although you often get eaten alive by mosquitos. This particular one was decent, a good mix of guys and girls from all different grades at school, and someone had Neil Young on the stereo.

I had slipped off into the darkness to take a leak, and was walking back to the fire when I ran into Summer, who was my friend Todd's girlfriend. Summer is short and pretty good-looking, black hair and a nose ring. She lives on a farm near where the bush party was being held, and she's a grade ahead of me. She has a reputation for being a bit of a nymphomaniac, but she and Todd had been going steady for over a year. I think I mentioned Todd before; he's the guy whose brother deals. Todd has scored with a lot of girls, so when I think about it now, it's a bit surprising that he had been steady with the same girl for so long. Todd drives one of those old VW Westphalia vans complete with a built-in icebox, which he keeps well stocked.

"Hey, Summer, where's Todd?"

"Oh, we just had a bit of an argument and he's gone off for a few minutes to cool down."

We chatted, mostly small talk. After a couple minutes I signaled with my body language that I'd like to go rejoin my friends at the fire, but Summer was making it equally clear she didn't want me to go, that she wanted to keep talking. In fact, she was interested in more than just talking, she was coming on to me, loud and clear. I wasn't interested. I mean, she's cute and all, but she and Todd weren't broken up and I don't try to cut in on my friends' relationships. And in any event, I was still infatuated with Eve at the time.

Summer wasn't taking my hint. She leaned in close to me and was just trying to put her arm around my waist when Todd came walking up. I thought for sure he would be pissed, but he wasn't. He just said,

"Hey guys, how's it going?"

Summer continued to squeeze in and got her arm all the way around me, while replying,

"I was just going to ask Landon to go for a walk with me."

Guess what Todd says?

"Sure, go for it. Don't let me stop you."

This was too weird for me. I unhooked myself from Summer's grip and made my way back to the fire. When I got there I saw Aadel, and asked him if he knew whether Todd and Summer had split up.

"Shit no. They're banging each other as often as they ever did."

Weird.

About half an hour later, Tiina showed up with a couple girl friends. Dale wasn't with her. She came over to say hello, and we got into a conversation about various things, like who was at the party, who was seeing who, and so on. I told her about my encounter earlier that night with Todd and Summer, finishing by asking her,

"Isn't it weird?"

Tiina's face got real angry looking, and she said,

"It's weirder than you think. Summer's pregnant, don't you know?"

No, I didn't know, and neither did any of my friends so far as I was aware. I asked,

"Does Todd know?"

"Of course he does, stupid. Don't you know he's been trying to raise money to pay for the abortion?"

I guess I am pretty stupid, because I didn't know that either.

"Well if she's pregnant, why was she hitting on me tonight? Why would Todd not mind?"

"Think about it",

was all Tiina said, and she walked away.

I actually didn't think much about it. It was turning out to be a really good party, a lot more people turned up than were originally expected, and everyone was cool and laid back. I hate those parties where you get a couple yahoos who whoop it up too much and start fights or are generally so obnoxious everyone else leaves early. That didn't happen. Some people spend a whole party hanging around with their closest buddies but I'm more the mingling type, and this was a good party for mingling. I ran into a number of people I hadn't seen in a long time and caught up with what they were doing. Like one guy that I used to play soccer with as a kid, Scott, who had gotten into serious trouble in the sixth grade (I'm can't remember exactly what happened, it was probably drugs) and so his parents make him go to a private school the next town over. The school is run by some Christian group, and even though his family isn't religious, his folks thought sending him there would straighten him out. I guess it sort of has, since he was telling me he's getting good grades and is captain of the soccer team, and the team is pretty good. On the other hand, he can't say a single sentence without lacing it with a lot of unnecessary f-bombs. I can't imagine the Christians taught him that.

Scott showed me this crazy tatt that he got. It must have cost him a fortune. It takes up half his back and it looks almost exactly like the cover of the *Bat Out of Hell* album by Meat Loaf, you know the one with the naked guy exploding out of a graveyard on a chopper while a giant bat screeches from the church steeple? The only difference is that, in the tatt, the naked biker looks exactly like Scott. It is hysterical. Scott told me that the gym teacher saw it when the team was changing for soccer, and he went ballistic and told the principal that Scott ought to be expelled, but the school needs the tuition money so they let him off with a warning. Scott was killing himself laughing as he retold the story of how he sat with a straight face in front of the principal and solemnly promised that he would never, ever get another Meat Loaf tattoo again. When I asked him what his parents thought of the ink, he just shrugged, and said,

"They really don't give a shit what I do as long as I don't embarrass them in public. They're too into themselves."

After an hour or so of mingling I got back to the place near the fire where I started, and was thinking about heading home since Eve clearly wasn't going to show up. I saw Aadel again, who said,

"You missed it."

"Missed what?"

"Tiina and Summer were going at it."

"What do you mean, 'going at it'?"

"I didn't hear it all, especially when it first started, but about half an hour ago Summer was standing over near Todd's van, and Tiina came storming out of nowhere and just started tearing into her, giving her shit for something. I honestly thought she was going to start throwing some punches at her. Summer was scared shitless, and was yelling, 'I didn't, I didn't'."

"Didn't what?"

"I don't know dude, but the last thing I heard Tiina say to her was, 'You just stay away from Landon, you scheming bitch'. And then she left the party."

Aadel looked at me for an explanation. I didn't say anything. Then he asked,

"Are you and Tiina finally getting together? Dale will be pissed if you are. Or have you been boning Summer on the side? Todd will be pissed if you are. Either way, you'll be pissing someone off."

"No man, I don't know anything about any of this. I saw Summer and Todd when I first got here, but before tonight I hadn't seen Summer except at school. She's into Todd. And I haven't been seeing Tiina, either. She's into Dale, you know that."

"Well, Tiina was into you before she was into Dale."

Aadel was getting ready to leave, so I hitched a ride back to town with him and his brother and a couple other guys, four of us wedged in the back seat. Later that night, lying in my bed, I couldn't sleep. I'm like that whenever I've been at a party or a dance, I end up lying in a semi-awake state for hours, feeling like I'm still at the party, going over the events in my mind. So I was lying there, thinking about that weird encounter with Summer, where it seemed pretty evident that she wanted to get together with me, even though I'd hardly spoken a half dozen sentences to her in my life, and even though she's still Todd's girlfriend and, apparently, pregnant. And then Todd wandered along and seemed to be encouraging it. And then after Tiina heard what happened she went crazy on Summer. None of it made any sense. Unless...

Remember how I told you when I was a kid I liked to read Hardy Boy mysteries? I still like mysteries, and now I'm totally addicted to Sherlock Holmes stories. Have you ever read any? You ought to. I've read them all, most of them several times. In one of them, Holmes explains to Watson that once you've eliminated all other possibilities, whatever explanation remains must be the truth, no matter how unlikely it seems. After puzzling it over for a long time in my bed that night, the only explanation that remained in the mysterious case of my encounter with Todd and Summer is that I was to be their dupe. They needed money so that Summer could get an abortion. She must have been early enough in her pregnancy that she wasn't showing, and not many guys knew, including me. So maybe they figured that if Summer could convince me to have sex with her, she could later tell me that I got her pregnant, and then she could pressure me to cough up some money for the abortion. Me being a nice guy and from a family with a bit of money, I would make a good target for such a scheme. Tiina, knowing all the facts, quickly deduced what Summer and Todd were up to, and confronted Summer to make sure her little plan would not succeed. She was Sherlock Holmes, coming to my rescue.

But who wants to think of himself as a dupe? Just before I finally fell asleep, I came up with a more satisfactory solution: Summer is a harmless nympho who simply wanted to get it on with me because I'm a real stud, and Todd wasn't able to get it up for her once she got pregnant because he was too worried about finding money, and Tiina was simply acting jealous because she is still hot for me.

Yeah. That sounds a lot better.

## Chapter 9: Leah's orbit

After the bush party things really started getting weird for me. Everyone at school was talking about how Summer and Tiina had been fighting over me. That, plus Eve's rumor that she had slept with me and my fight with Eddie Murphy over Mara, meant that I was starting to get a reputation as being a bit of a ladies' man. That can be a bit dangerous, because there's always some ugly bully who doesn't get much attention from the ladies and will vent his frustration by pounding on a loverboy. But ever since I had stood up to Eddie Murphy after the high school dance, the would-be bullies had left me alone, and even the Vandenfarts seemed to have lost interest in me lately.

Like I said, it's weird. Because, as you know, I had never so much as kissed either Eve or Summer, and hadn't done much more than kiss Tiina on one occasion. And you know that my confrontation with Eddie Murphy was not exactly an Ultimate Warrior throw-down, and that I hadn't done anything more than dance with Mara once. But hey, if you can get through high school without anyone rocking your boat, it's a good thing. And I was doing better than that. I won't ever win any popularity contests or be voted class president, but I can honestly say that some kids were starting to think I was reasonably cool, and those that didn't think I was cool at least had some respect for me.

None of this made me any less lonely. Lonely? Yes, lonely. I don't like to admit it now, but I had gotten to feeling sorry for myself a lot. I know I had no right to. I have friends, guys and girls, and have never been short of things to do or people to hang out with. I can walk down the hallway during class change and say, "hey" to lots of people. But the truth is, I had never really felt any strong connection to anyone else at school except Eve, who didn't seem to feel the same way about me, and was hard to figure out. Disconnected – that's the word that best describes what I was feeling. I still am sort of disconnected. I hope it doesn't make you think any less of me, I'm just trying to be honest with you. I can guess what you're thinking: Suck it up, lots of people have far worse problems. And you're right, so I'll stop whining and get on with my story.

The week after the bush party our social studies teacher asked me one day to stay after class. Other than talking a little too much in class, I couldn't imagine what I might have done wrong. I figured I was on track for at least an A grade. He was a pretty cool teacher and I liked the subject a lot. As it turned out, the reason he kept me behind was to ask me if I would join the team that would represent our school at the regional United Nations Assembly the following month. I didn't know exactly what he was talking about, since it's something students typically do when they are in their senior year, and I hadn't ever given it any thought. It took a few minutes for the teacher to explain to me what would be involved, and I'll try to explain it to you here as simply as I can.

Each year all the schools in our county and the next two over select teams of six student representatives for a pretend UN Assembly meeting. Each school gets assigned a different UN country to represent. The organizers select a topic that is of big international importance, like nuclear weapons or AIDS or terrorism. Each UN team has to research their assigned country's position on the topic, and then all the school teams meet for two days at the university campus to negotiate an international treaty to deal with the problem. It's obviously not the real United Nations, but the organizers try to make it feel as real as possible, the idea being to get students interested in global issues. It's not a bad idea. Most of my friends don't pay any attention to global issues, unless you consider the X-Games a global issue.

It sounded pretty cool to me, but I told the teacher I was a little hesitant because I thought it was something that students only did in their senior year, and even then it was only the brainiacs who were chosen. He replied,

"That's usually the case, Landon, but I can see that you're just putting in time at school and are not being challenged. You're more worldly than most of our students your age, and certainly more worldly than most of our seniors this year. This will be good for you."

Which was a funny thing to say, since 'worldly' is not a word I would use to describe someone who has spent his entire life in Not-Sedro-Woolley. But he was right about me just putting in my time.

He then went on to say that it would be a big commitment and that I shouldn't say yes right away but should think about it. Then he named the people who were already on the team and when he said Leah's name, I didn't need to hear anything more.

"I'm in."

And that was how I became part of Leah's orbit.

The following week the UN team started meeting every day after school. It was me, Leah, and four senior students I recognized from passing them in the hall. They were clearly the type for whom school is all business, who work their asses off for A+ grades so they can win a university scholarship. At our first meeting the teacher made us introduce ourselves, and then he explained how this year's UN conference theme was climate change, and that the goal was to negotiate a binding international treaty to reduce greenhouse gas emissions. That sounded pretty interesting, since environmental sustainability is something that I'm into.

Our school was assigned the role of China, which is also pretty cool. I'm always interested in learning about China since it seems like everything we buy these days is made there. When I think of China, I imagine it to be a flat, treeless country covered with millions of big old factories with assembly lines churning out every kind of thing imaginable. When you were a kid did you ever read *The Lorax* by Dr Seuss? It's a book where this creep called the Once-ler invents some useless piece of shit called a thneed and sells them to morons who will buy anything, and he builds an enormous factory and cuts down every last truffula tree to make thneeds and when he's done the place is a wildlife-less wasteland. That's what I imagine China looks like, a treeless waste covered with thneed factories. But we shouldn't blame the Chinese for making thneeds, we should blame ourselves for being the morons stupid enough to buy thneeds.

I hope you understand what I mean when I talk about greenhouse gas emissions. If you do, skip ahead to the next paragraph. If not, here's a quick explanation: The Earth gets most of its energy from the sun. The sun is very hot, obviously, and the energy shoots out in certain wavelengths: mostly visible light, some infrared light (you know, the stuff you can only see with night vision goggles) and ultraviolet light (the stuff that gives you skin cancer if you don't wear sunscreen). Some of the sun's energy that reaches the Earth reflects straight back into space, off shiny surfaces like snow and the hoods of silver Camaros. Some of the energy gets absorbed by dark objects, like the ground and forests and the top of your head and the hoods of black Camaros. Energy that gets absorbed will later get re-emitted back into the air (hold your hand over the hood of a black Camaro on a hot day and you'll feel it) and will eventually escape to outer space. The amount of energy coming into the atmosphere has to be balanced by the same amount of energy being re-emitted back into space. Otherwise, the Earth would quickly get super hot (if the absorbed energy is not re-emitted) or super cold (if too much energy gets re-emitted). But it stays balanced. One important thing that happens is that the re-emitted energy is a different wavelength from the incoming energy from the sun. That's because trees, your head, black Camaros, etc are not as hot as the sun. When the re-emitted energy tries to leave our atmosphere, carbon dioxide in the air (the stuff plants breathe in) slows it down and tries to prevent it from escaping to outer space. It eventually does escape, but the carbon dioxide causes that re-emitted energy to linger in the atmosphere longer than it otherwise would, and so temperatures at the Earth's surface are warmer than they would be if there were no carbon dioxide in the air. Scientists call carbon dioxide a 'greenhouse gas' because it acts like glass in a greenhouse, which lets sunlight in but prevents the heat from escaping. There are lots of different greenhouse gases; carbon dioxide is just the most common one.

People all around the world are creating more and more carbon dioxide and other greenhouse gases, which happens when you burn fossil fuels or cut down a lot of trees. Scientists are warning that if we don't stop, the Earth is going to heat up to dangerous levels and we'll all be fucked. But no one seems to be paying attention, everyone just keeps driving more cars and buying more thneeds that need to be shipped from China. It's all gimme, gimme, gimme, more, more, more. No country produces more greenhouse gases than China, which isn't surprising since everything's made there. To power all those millions of thneed factories China burns a shitload of coal, creating a shitload of carbon dioxide. But the real source of the problem is rich countries like the US and Canada. America's greenhouse gas emissions are almost as high as China's except there's three times more people in China, and in China workers only earn like twenty or thirty bucks a day, and not many of them have cars or big homes or any of that stuff we have. China says it's willing to reduce its greenhouse gas emissions, but only if the US will do the same. It will cost China a lot to switch from coal to solar panels and wind turbines and other clean sources of energy, so they don't plan to do it unless the US does, too. Can you blame them?

I learned this stuff and a lot more as I helped our team prepare. It's pretty cool that our school got to represent one of the most important countries in the UN debate. The whole thing was a great experience. The seniors treated me as a totally equal team member, even though I was still only a sophomore. They didn't order me around or assign me all the grunt work like photocopying stuff, the way I thought they would. That's what happens on sports teams. The young players get hazed and have to do all the grunt stuff like carry equipment bags while the older players laugh. On the UN team, the work was split six equal ways. We met every day for an hour after school for two weeks. We had brainstorming sessions, where everyone gave their ideas on things we could do, and the others respected my opinion. We set up our own work schedule and by the time the UN Assembly meeting arrived we were totally ready for it. I knew more about China than anyone else in Not-Sedro-Woolley, with the exception of my five teammates.

When the big day arrived the social studies teacher drove us to the university campus in his minivan. I had never been there before. I was pretty intimidated by the big glass buildings and the lawns and the university students, who were all old and cool and good-looking. Well, most of them, anyhow. I'd like to tell you everything that happened, but the two days we spent in those UN meeting rooms were a blur. We had decided that two of our team members would do all the talking on behalf of our team, and neither of them was Leah or me. She and I were given the responsibility of doing instant research on any proposals the other teams might bring up during the negotiations that our team wasn't familiar with. You know the old saying, "You don't know what you don't know". We figured the other teams would start bringing up lots of stuff we didn't know about other countries' greenhouse gas emissions policies or different scientific opinions on the best plan of action or things like that. Whenever that happened, Leah and I would be expected to figure out as quickly as possible what China's response would be, and advise our other team members what to say. As it turned out, our team was ten times better prepared than any of the other schools, and we totally kicked their asses. The two students speaking on behalf of our team totally dominated the negotiations.

By the mid-morning break of the first day, it was already clear there wouldn't be as much for Leah and me to do as we thought. The other team members suggested we rotate our roles, so that all of us could take turns doing the speaking and negotiating, but I didn't want to. I was happy staying in the background. Leah felt the same. During the lunch break that first day, we were all in a good mood, because we were, as I said, kicking ass. We were all laughing and talking about the other schools' teams, how the team representing the US was a bunch of dumb-asses, how the team representing the Europeans was smart but the person speaking for their team was too quiet and let herself get talked over by the other teams, and stuff like that. I suggested to my teammates that we could help the European team by telling all the other teams to stop interrupting the European team, since they were the only ones even close to being as well prepared as us. My teammates agreed, and so for the rest of the next day and a half, China and Europe ended up dominating, and we wrote almost the entire agreement that came out of the negotiations.

I know it sounds like I am totally geeking out on this UN assembly thing, but I don't give a shit. It was a total rush to be involved in something where a group of people pulled together and achieved excellence. It's the first and last time it ever happened to me. At the conclusion of the assembly on the second day, a university professor who was an expert on climate change and had been observing our negotiations stood up and gave her opinion on what had taken place. She awarded medals to the two teams she thought did the best job representing their respective countries. To no one's surprise, China and Europe got the medals. The only real surprise was that only four members were there from the Chinese team to accept their medals, because at that moment Leah and I were in an empty lecture hall licking each other's tonsils.

I'm still not entirely sure how that came to happen. Over the course of those two days, we were just always at each other's side. On the first morning we maintained the usual amount of physical space you give to other people and reserve for yourself, but with each passing hour that amount was continually shrinking. When we ate lunch on the second day in the university cafeteria with the rest of our teammates, Leah and I sat so close to one another on the bench that our legs were rubbing and our shoulders often touched. Just as the afternoon break was about to start that second day, Leah said, "Let's go for a walk instead." So we ditched our teammates without telling them, and went outside. We didn't walk very fast. It seemed like Leah wanted to talk about something important, but couldn't bring herself to do it. I was too terrified to say a word, I didn't want to ruin this. I was afraid that if I opened my mouth, she might realize I was just some inconsequential sophomore twerp who was in total awe of her, and she'd turn around and walk back inside.

So the two of us just walked along in silence, side by side. She reached out and took my hand. We continued to walk along like that, hand in hand. I saw people looking at us kind of funny. One of the rules about the UN assembly is that you have to dress the part, so I was wearing a shirt and tie and dress pants, and Leah was wearing a white blouse, black skirt, nylons, and pumps. Not exactly how university students dress to go to class, if you haven't noticed. I felt like I was holding hands with a goddess. There had been many times I tried to imagine what Leah would look like if she wasn't wearing that awful McD's uniform or the baggy sweats she wore to school each day. To be honest, I'd mostly tried to imagine her naked. I hadn't realized how stunning she would look when dressed like someone going for a job interview.

If there was any thought going through my head it was that I wished the university campus would stretch on for a hundred miles, so that we would never have to stop walking. I was under a spell and didn't want it to be broken. But of course, university campuses, like all things, must come to an end. We reached a parking lot, and that was it, no more campus to walk across in that direction. There was a red brick building off to the left, with a sign saying "Environmental Studies " over the door.

"Come on",

she said. We entered, walked down the corridor until we found an empty lecture hall with an unlocked door. We went inside, sat in the back row and held one another. After a while, we started kissing. We didn't go any farther than that. After all, we were in a strange place where anyone could have walked in at anytime, although no one did.

We were in there for almost an hour. We both knew when it was time to go back, and we did. As you would expect, our teammates had surprised looks on their faces when we rejoined them a few minutes after the medals had been awarded. The closing reception was going on, and everyone from all the teams was drinking pop and eating snacks and mingling. Leah and I were totally cool. We walked up and joined in the conversation like we had never been away and nothing had happened. We smiled and introduced ourselves to the other teams, and agreed with everyone who was saying that it was a great learning experience, and how solid it would be to actually work as a diplomat or a UN official for your career. The European delegation was hanging out with our team, and they were all thanking us for being so cool and helping them separate themselves from the other schools that weren't taking things seriously enough.

One of the most amazing moments of my life happened then. Leah was talking to one of the girls from the European team as I was chatting to one of the guys from that same team, and I glanced over at her. Leah had begun to radiate. I'm not kidding. Late afternoon sunlight was streaming in through the big glass windows of the reception hall and, I swear, it was seeking her out, to shine on her first. She must have sensed I was staring at her. She turned, and smiled, and then...

Actually, I'm not sure what happened then. I suppose a bunch of other shit must have happened, and I guess the reception must have come to an end and I must have ridden home in the teacher's minivan and I guess I ate some dinner and talked to my parents and showed them my medal... or maybe not. I don't know. Our solar system consists of the sun and eight planets (nine if you count Pluto, which isn't really a planet), but most of it consists of the nothingness in between. Everything that happened after that smile from Leah merged into the same sort of nothingness. For the remainder of the day, she was my sun. I stayed awake late into the night, trying to put off the inevitable moment when the light must fade, which it did.

## Chapter 10: An olive-sided flycatcher

The next morning was a Saturday. I'm not usually an early riser – what teenager is? – but it was barely 6 am and, despite having had no more than a couple hours sleep, I was wide awake. Man, did I feel good. I was in Nirvana. Not the band, but the state of purity of thought, the state of tranquility and absolute inner peace that followers of Eastern religions seek to achieve. I looked at the ceiling, thinking of Leah, of course. It's hard to put precisely into words my thoughts at that moment, the best I can say is that I was enjoying inner peace.

Then, BANG, something hit my bedroom window. I got up, opened it, and looked down. There was a bird lying on the ground, dead, its neck broken. I went outside in my bare feet. The sun had only just come up, the air was cool, and there was dew on the grass. I picked up the bird and looked at it for a long time. It wasn't super colorful or anything, and wasn't much bigger than a sparrow, but it didn't look like any other birds I had seen in our yard before. A day or two later, I looked it up in my dad's Audubon Society field guide to birds and learned it was an olive-sided flycatcher. This type of bird doesn't hang out at bird feeders like sparrows or cardinals or blue jays do. It fends for itself, eating insects. It spends winters in South America and summers in the western mountains or the forests of northern Canada. It must have been passing through Not-Sedro-Woolley on a journey to someplace else. I looked up and saw that the red light of the sun's early morning rays was reflecting off my window at an unusual angle. The bird had likely been blinded by the light and flown straight into the glass. I wondered if the bird had realized its mistake at the last moment, or if its final thought was only of the brilliant light all around it.

I brought the bird into my room and laid it on my desk. The house was quiet, there was no one else up. I sat on the edge of my bed and texted Leah,

*When can I C U?*

Almost right away came the reply,

*Come now.*

That was easier said than done. As I mentioned before, Leah lives in a farm out on the edge of town, at the opposite side of Not-Sedro-Woolley. I don't have a car, and the public transit system in our town sucks. I texted back,

*On my way 2 bus.*

I brushed my teeth, put on some deodorant to cover up the teenage-boy smell and a baseball cap to cover up the bedhead, grabbed my skateboard, and dashed out the door. I had to skate for several blocks and wait about twenty minutes until a bus came. Because it was still early, there was only one other person on the bus, a Filipina lady in nurses' scrubs who must have been on her way home at the end of a night shift. She looked tired, but was still polite enough to smile when we made eye contact as I was taking a seat. No one else got on until we got downtown, where I hopped off and waited another ten minutes until I could transfer to the bus that ran out towards Leah's house. I rode it to the end of the line. This time I was the only person riding and, even though I deliberately chose a seat near the rear door, the driver wanted to chat. He hollered over the noise of the bus,

"Great day for baseball."

I hollered back,

"Yeah."

I should have just ignored him – I was wanting to close my eyes and think about Leah – but you never know in Not-Sedro-Woolley. He might be the father or uncle of someone I know, or maybe he knows my teachers, or whatever, and word would get back that I was rude to him. I tend to be polite to everyone anyhow, so after I said Yeah, he took it as an invitation to start yakking about the New York Yankees, and whether they would be back in the playoffs again this year. As if I gave two shits. Baseball is only slightly less boring than curling, and from what I know of them (which, admittedly, isn't much) the New York Yankees aren't very likeable. But I suppose if you're driving the bus up and down the same streets every day, you've got to pass the time thinking of something, so why not baseball? While the driver was rattling on about the Yankees, I nodded and occasionally shouted Yeah, and started daydreaming that if I were a bus driver, I'd pretty quickly get fed up with my job and would probably snap one day. When that day came I'd gun the accelerator and shout at the passengers, "Sit back you bastards and enjoy the ride, 'cause we're headed to Sedro-Woolley today!"

I wouldn't stop at the end of my regularly scheduled route, I'd continue straight on to Leah's house, stop long enough to pick her up and let out any passengers too afraid to come with us. Then I'd point that big silver bus westbound, drive off into the sunset and before you know it...

"Last stop. End of the line."

What? I must have really been daydreaming. I walked up to the front door, thanked the driver and wished his Yankees well, then skated the last half mile to Leah's house.

I had seen her place many times from my parents' car as we drove by, but I'd never been past the gate. The house, which was near the road, looked kind of like any other brick house built in the 1970s. The front yard was well kept. There were a couple cars at the side of the house. Practical ones, I think Toyotas or Hondas, and an older Chevy pick-up truck. There was a laneway that ran past the house and down into a small farmyard, with an undersized barn and some paddocks, chicken coops, and sheds. There were beehives along the left side of the small barn, and a small orchard of fruit trees on a slope farther on. I saw Leah come out of the barn. She saw me, set down a pail she was carrying, and waved. As I walked down the lane, the stinky sweet smell of manure came into my nose. I don't mind that smell. At certain times of the year the farmers south and west of town apply manure to their cornfields, and the odor comes drifting into Not-Sedro-Woolley on the wind. A couple stupid old geezers regularly complain to city hall and to the local newspaper, demanding that the mayor do something to make it stop, that the smell is so bad they can't leave their windows open on a warm evening. But there's nothing the mayor can do. Farmers have a right to farm, and manure is good fertilizer. If you don't like the smell of farm manure, move to New York, I say. I bet they've got some real nice smells coming off the streets there on a warm evening. You can even catch a Yankees game any time you want.

Leah was wearing a pair of baggy old sweats, a green hoodie, and rubber boots. Not the stylish Hunter rubber boots the preppy girls buy at the mall, but the cheap and practical black ones with red soles they sell at the TSC store. TSC stands for Tractor Supply Company, in case you didn't know, and as its name suggests, they sell mostly stuff that farmers need. Her hair hadn't been brushed, and a few bits of straw were clinging to it. If you were seeing her for the first time, you might not think much of her. But for me, those old work clothes could not hide the woman who had radiated at last night's reception. This is what my Cinderella looked like the day after the ball, and I liked it.

I said,

"Hey".

"Hey, Landon."

"Can I help you with something?"

"No, thanks, I'm pretty much done. The only thing left to do is sweep out the henhouse, and I don't think you're dressed for it."

I looked down – shorts, sandals, t-shirt, my skateboard under my arm.

"I guess not, not really. And I don't know how to do it."

"No problem, you can watch. Talk to me while I'm doing it. Tell me what you liked best about the UN conference."

She got to work while I started telling her about how I found it amazing that our team and the European team were able to get so much done, even though we were surrounded by a much larger number of stupid and under-prepared groups. Which was a lie, of course. I mean, the parts about us getting a lot done and the other groups being stupid were true, but it was a lie to say it was what I like best about the conference. Being with Leah was obviously the best thing. She finished sweeping, clouds of dust floating in the air around her, and said,

"Surrounded by stupid and under-prepared people. That sounds like life in general. Could you please pass me that pail?"

Which I did. It had some straw in the bottom. She ducked into the back part of the henhouse and came out with a dozen eggs in the pail. I don't think I'd ever seen fresh eggs before. I held one. It was warm to the touch. Leah said,

"One of the benefits of living on a farm – fresh eggs for breakfast every day."

"I thought eggs were bad for you, too much cholesterol. I think you're only supposed to eat the whites."

"That's the silly stuff city people say. There's nothing healthier than whole eggs, humans have been eating them forever. Hey, come on, don't look so embarrassed. I'm not making fun of you. You can't help that you never lived on a farm, even a little bitty one like this that isn't much of a farm at all. Let's go sit on that bench over there by the barn. We've got stuff to talk about."

We sat down. The bench was in the sun. Leah put the pail of eggs in a bit of shade nearby. I tossed my skateboard down next to it. She showed me her hands – they were a little dirty, as you might expect.

"Still want to hold them today?"

she laughed. I laughed too, and took the one closest to me, her right hand, and held it between my own, my right hand on top of hers, my left one under it.

"I lied. Just then. You asked me to say what I liked best about the UN conference. You were what I liked best."

"I know."

"And you?"

I asked, hopefully. She said,

"Ah, that's complicated. First, let me start by saying that I like you, Landon. I like you a lot. You are not like any of the other boys around this town. And when I say 'boys', I do mean boys. This town is full of boys. Not just the school. The guys here never grow up, even after high school is over. My brother Brent is an obvious example, but there's plenty more like him. They have no aspirations, no thoughts about what goes on in the wider world, no curiosity about why things are the way they are, no ideas to make things better. No understanding of what it means to be a man or how to at least act like one. You are a man, Landon. You have so many of those good qualities and, best of all, you don't realize it. Or, if you do, you don't make a big deal about it. I mean, you do still need to fill out a bit and grow a little more hair on your face before you're physically a man, but emotionally, intellectually, you're already there."

I was blushing pretty badly, and starting to sweat a little, too. She continued,

"There, you're getting embarrassed again. Don't be. Just as you can't help not being a farmer, you can't help being younger than me. But don't worry, I think you're beautiful, and when you're finished filling out in a couple years, I'll want to fuck your brains out, often, if you'll let me. But you will have to accept starting right now that you and I won't ever have a romantic relationship. I can't be your girlfriend, and I never will be."

My throat got tight, and even though I haven't cried since I was in the first grade, I had to concentrate hard to keep my voice strong and not spontaneously burst into tears. I asked,

"Why not?"

"Well, first of all, I have a boyfriend, Luke Philps."

As soon as she said it, I thought, I should have *known* she'd have a boyfriend. How could she possibly not? And I wasn't surprised it was Luke. Luke is a tall, blonde, easygoing guy who lives on a farm and works part time at the dairy.

"Luke and I started dating when we were sixteen, and I expect that after we finish college we'll get married and start our own farm somewhere near town, as soon as we can afford to. Luke is a great guy, he's steady and strong and he adores me, and that makes me feel wonderful. He's going to college to study horticulture, and he has ideas about growing high-value crops in small spaces that could potentially revolutionize farming in this region. I start college in September and I plan to become a veterinarian. Between the two of us, we will make a heck of a team. That's our plan, to get ourselves a farm, run it successfully, and live close to family and friends. That's a good life, Landon, and I want it.

But sometimes at night, I imagine what it would be like to be a different person, with a different future. I have this dream that comes often, in which I live in Washington or London or Paris, and I work as a political advisor to the President or an ambassador or something like that. It changes each time I dream that dream. But I'm always someone whose job it is to understand the important issues of the day, and to use that knowledge to influence world leaders. In the dream I'm a woman who is glamorous and successful, not because of the way she looks, the way movie stars are, but because she is intelligent and thoughtful, and people listen to her opinion on things that really matter. Whenever I wake up from that dream I fantasize about what it would be like to work and socialize with people who are intelligent and worldly. I imagine we'd have long, passionate conversations about how to change the world for the better, and we'd have the confidence to try and pull it off. If I were able to be two people at once, that's who the other me would be."

I was staring at Leah all wide-eyed, and I think my mouth was hanging open a bit. I'd never heard anyone talk like that before, I'd never had anyone share their secret dreams with me. It's a very cool sensation, and I still get a bit of a rush when I think about it. I'm getting a rush right now just writing it down. Anyhow, Leah paused, and looked at me looking at her, and said,

"The UN assembly was a chance for me to play out my fantasy. Those weeks of research we did, all that hard work preparing for it, and then on the two days of the conference all of us working in sync and becoming the most important team of all the schools that were there, and making the others agree to something we came up with. I know it was all pretend, but it is as close as I'll ever get to the real thing, and I enjoyed it very much."

"OK, but how did I fit in? What happened yesterday afternoon? You know, the walk, the, uh... holding each other?"

"Oh Landon, you don't get it, do you? It wouldn't have felt as real if you hadn't been part of it. You've got this dream of leaving here and going out into the bigger world, and unlike me, you will follow that dream through to the end. I know you will. You'll leave and you'll make something of yourself somewhere else, and you'll do great things that would never happen if you stayed here. There are so many possibilities waiting for you in this Sedro-Woolley place that you talk about, or whatever it's called, I bet you can't even imagine them all. For you, the world beyond here is not a fantasy or a dream, it is a reality that is on the verge of happening. It's only a question of when. There is no Sedro-Woolley in my future. My reality is here, and always will be. But the last two days, I got to live out my alternative future, where I went out into the wider world, too, with you, and we were going achieve great things together. Did you see all those college students stare at us as we walked across their campus? They were just these little worker bees buzzing off to their classes or whatever, wondering about us two hot-looking, dead cool people who were clearly taking a break from something far more interesting than a first year psych lecture. And when we went into that dark lecture hall, I don't know what you were thinking and I don't want to know, but while I was holding you I had my eyes closed and was letting my imagination go crazy. I imagined we were two diplomats sitting on a plane, flying across the Atlantic to Paris, where we would go for a walk along the Seine before dashing off to dinner with the British Prime Minister, who had flown in from London just to meet us, and then after dinner we'd go back to our hotel and I wouldn't want to go back to my room but to yours, and I'd tell you to order up a bottle of champagne and... I guess that's when I started kissing you for real. It sounds totally insane now, I know. Now you probably think I'm crazy. I wouldn't blame you if you got up and ran away screaming, to get as far away from me as you can."

She smiled, kind of. I didn't know what to say. I mean, would you have been able to think of exactly the right thing to say at a moment like that? If you could, I sure could have used your help then. Looking back, I now know what I should have said was, "I don't think you're crazy, I am honored you trusted me enough to share this with me, and it's made me fall even more deeply in love with you, and I want so desperately to be your boyfriend I'd give up my silly dreams of going west in a heartbeat, please just ditch Luke and let me be the guy you start a farm with, even if I don't know how to be a farmer, I'd learn, I'd do whatever it takes, or maybe better yet you could come west to Sedro-Woolley with me, I'm sure they've got great farms there and we could get one, we could leave right now, just please don't cut me loose..."

But I didn't. I did start to say,

"I don't think you're crazy..."

and then I said the stupidest thing ever,

"...and even if you don't want to be boyfriend-girlfriend, I'd still like to be your friend."

That's it. What was I thinking? Seriously, *what the fuck* was I thinking? I should have just blurted out all my feelings right there, no matter how muddled they might have come out. What did I have to lose? We would have still been friends either way, right?

Leah leaned over and gave me a good kiss square on the mouth, and said,

"Thank you. No hard feelings?"

"No, only good feelings,"

I stood up and grabbed my skateboard.

"I guess I'd better go. I'll see you at school on Monday."

"See you."

As I walked back up the lane past her house, Leah's brother Brent was standing in the open doorway, eating a bowl of Fruit Loops in his jammies. He said,

"Hey, skaterboy. I saw you kissing Farmer Brown back there by the barn. Woo, woo, woo, aren't you the stud. Why didn't you take her for a roll in the hay? I bet she takes it alpaca-style."

"Fuck off, Brent."

"I recognize you. You're that Landon kid. Your mom's a babe, which is pretty impressive given how many puppies she squeezed out. You tell her anytime she wants a piece of this, she knows where to find me," he said, grabbing at his dick. I never even bothered to look back and acknowledge him.

When I got back to the road, I realized I couldn't face another encounter with the talkative bus driver, so I rode my board the entire way home. It took almost an hour and a half. My dad was in the garden, picking some Japanese beetles off his roses. He waved as I went inside. Mom was in the kitchen, making toast for my younger sisters.

"Hi Landon, you were out early this morning."

"Yeah, I just wanted to get in some skateboarding this morning, I've got a lot of things to do today."

I went up to my room. The olive-sided flycatcher was still lying there on my desk. Which of course it would be, it was dead, after all. I took a photo of it, which I saved as the wallpaper on my phone.

## Chapter 11: An ending, of sorts

I wish there was some really dramatic way to finish this story, some Hollywood ending to it, but there isn't. I thought about making one up. One of my ideas was an ending where on the skateboard ride back from Leah's house I was so deep in my thoughts that I didn't see the bus coming, the one being driven by that guy who loved the Yankees, and it hit me and my neck was broken, and I ended up trapped in a wheelchair, and could never go to the real Sedro-Woolley. If it ended that way, you'd feel so sorry for me and think, isn't it ironic that Landon broke his neck just like the olive-sided flycatcher. Or maybe you wouldn't get the symbolism of the bird, and just think, it figures that the bus driver was a Yankees fan. And you'd be dying to know how Leah took the news about my broken neck. Would she be sad? Would she feel guilty? Would she break up with Luke and vow to spend the rest of her life with me, as my nurse/lover? And how would I react? Would I forgive her? Would I be grateful? Would there be a happy ever after? Or would I be angry at the rotten cards life dealt me, and push away everyone who ever loved me, and die alone, miserable?

And you would have believed that Hollywood-type of ending because you are conditioned to believe stuff like that. Stories don't get published and TV shows don't get screened unless there's a really memorable final chapter, one that keeps you on the edge of your seat to the very end. There has to be a tragedy, followed by some sort of redemption, and the hero has to overcome adversity to save the day and get the girl (or get the guy, if the hero is a heroine, but they don't make many movies like that). Even better is when the heroic climax is followed by some sort of moral play, a life-lesson can be taken away and discussed with friends over coffee at Starbucks. Like at the end of *Casablanca*, when Bogart puts Ingrid Bergman on the plane to America to go live in safety with her husband, while he stays behind to join the French resistance and fight Nazis. People eat that shit up. But I don't have a good enough imagination to come up with a dramatic ending like that. At least, not one good enough that you'd believe it. So I'll just tell you the truth, and let this story end with that.

Tomorrow's the first day of school again, first day of my junior year. I'm still in Not-Sedro-Woolley, still dreaming of heading west to the real one. I realized I need to start saving some money if I'm going to make it happen. There's no way my folks are going to be able to afford to send all of us kids to college or university, and I'm going to have to pay for a big chunk of it myself. So this past summer I started my first real job, cleaning the toilets at a rest stop out on the highway for two bucks an hour more than minimum wage. I'm going to keep working weekends and a few evening hours throughout the school year, and they'll pay me an extra buck an hour if I do.

I don't mind working. I mean, sure, there are days when I don't look forward to it, when I'd rather be hanging out at the park skateboarding or sitting in a coffee shop reading a book. I don't get to see my friends as much as I used to, obviously, since I'm at work so much. When I do get together with them, they joke about it, and say how they're going to ride out to the rest stop when I'm working, and all take enormous shits and not flush, just to watch me have to clean up all the stalls. Fortunately they're too lazy to do something like that. And I don't care if I have to clean up other people's shit to make money. Any job is a good job if you can get it.

Tiina works at the rest stop, too, serving bad coffee and stale muffins to minvanloads of families and traveling salesmen and bleary-eyed truckers. The truckers call her 'cutie' and things like that, but they're mostly harmless, and they tip her. It's the middle-aged men with neckties and wedding bands and kids Tiina's age that creep her out when they get flirty, because she knows a lot of them aren't joking or harmless. There's usually two girls working at her counter, but when one is on her break, the other one is left alone. On more than one occasion Tiina has had to sneak behind the cappuccino machine and text me to come over because some creep in a necktie is hassling her. I wander over with a yellow Wet Floor sign and start mopping next to the creep. The creep usually gives me a dirty look and asks me why I don't go mop somewhere else, but eventually he gets the picture and leaves.

Tiina and I try to take our breaks at the same time. When the weather is good we sit out behind the rest stop, on a picnic table near the dumpsters. The traffic on the highway makes a continuous drone in the background, and we sit on the same side of the table, facing out to where the truckers park their rigs. We talk about what other people at school are doing, and I tell her about my family and she talks about her mom. Tiina has no brothers or sisters, and her dad skipped out on them when Tiina was five. He's an investment banker somewhere, go figure, and has never tried to get in touch with Tiina. It's his loss, he doesn't realize what a fantastic daughter he has. Her mom works as the financial controller down at city hall. She and her mom are tight, and I think all of that explains why Tiina is more mature than other teenagers. Tiina's a bit like Leah in that she doesn't care a whole lot what other people think of her, and she's not embarrassed to work at a job that requires you to wear an ugly polyester uniform.

Tiina asked me once about Leah. She had heard something about us making goo-goo eyes at one another during the UN assembly. I didn't tell Tiina everything that went on, I simply said that I had a crush on Leah but she didn't have one on me, and that I'd get over it. Which is true, except for the part about getting over it. I haven't yet, even though Leah's now gone off to university. University girls do not date high school boys, period. I need to get my head around that. Tiina shrugged and said,

"Girls are like that. You'll find someone."

"But I'm not looking for anyone."

"Maybe someone is looking for you."

And then she moved on to another topic. Which is what I like about Tiina, she's so sensible.

What else can I tell you? I work, I skateboard, I try to get good grades at school. I now realize that within all of us there's a tension between wanting to fit in and wanting to distinguish ourselves from the crowd. I'm still trying to figure out the balance that's right for me. My family is pretty much the same as they were at the start of this story, just a bit older. Eve and her father moved back to California. I miss her. More than ever, I still plan to head west to the real Sedro-Woolley, as soon as I graduate from college and have some sort of skill I can make use of along the way. But sometimes, especially when I'm three-quarters of the way through a long shift cleaning toilets at the rest stop, I start feeling impatient, and want to get going west, now. I start getting panicky, like if I wait too long, I might never leave, or that the real Sedro-Woolley will no longer be there. And then the panic subsides and I resume mopping. So if you're ever driving west down the highway and pull over at the rest stop at... oops, I almost slipped up and gave away the real name of my hometown at the last minute. That would have been a mistake.

Let's just say that if you're driving along a highway somewhere and hit the rest stop for a break, and you see a skateboarder cleaning the toilets or mopping the floor, say hello. If he smiles shyly and keeps working, it could be me. If you want to be sure, just mention casually that you've got a long drive ahead of you to Sedro-Woolley. If he flinches, you'll know for sure it's me. And if you really are heading to Sedro-Woolley, give me five minutes to grab my things and I'll ride with you.


THE END

# Imagining #2: The Time Capsule

The Millennium Time Capsule was unearthed on March 11, 2009, the day ground was broken for the eagerly-anticipated expansion of the Pacific Verge Shopping Mall. The ceremony was attended by the usual assortment of local officials, Vice-Presidents of the Mall Corporation, and a smattering of employees of the Corporation who thought their attendance might be observed by their superiors and result in some undefined promotion to the lofty heights of mall middle-management.

It had been buried ten years previously, with considerably more interest and fanfare, on November 26th, 1999, the day after Thanksgiving. It was the busiest shopping day not only of the year but of the millennium. The time capsule had been lowered into a specially-designed chamber in the floor of the West Rotunda of the Mall. Local citizens had been encouraged to deposit small items of significance into the time capsule, which was to be unearthed in 2049 to show future citizens of Paisley, WA "the way we were" at the turn of the century. Unfortunately, mall expansion plans now called for the West Rotunda to be turned into an expanded food court, and the time capsule had to be unearthed to make way for the new floor drains.

The Mall Corporation had expanded into residential construction by the year 2009, and was currently developing detached, single family homes on the site of a former penitentiary near the Mall, the new neighborhood being called Pacific Verge Vista. The centerpiece of the new community was to be a 250 square-yard pentagonal green-space already marked out with survey stakes and named Time Capsule Park. In a specially designed underground chamber in the center of the grassy pentagon the relocated Millennium Time Capsule would rest for another 40 years.

It would be another 18 months before the park would be completed, so in the meantime the Millennium Time Capsule would rest safely in a storage locker behind the food court at the Mall. The Mall Corporation decided to take this opportunity to open the Time Capsule and add a few additional mementoes commemorating the birth of Pacific Verge Vista before resealing it and burying it at Time Capsule Park. A special notice ran in the Pacific Verge Shopping Mall Newsletter advising members of the public who had contributed items to the Millennium Time Capsule in 1999 that they could request the return of those items if their eagerness to reminisce about "the way we were" was so strong they could not wait until the next opening in 2049.

It therefore came to pass several weeks after the Unearthing Ceremony that Dale Douglas received an envelope from the Millennium Time Capsule Committee (c/o Pacific Verge Mall Corporation) containing a second envelope to which a form letter had been attached, reading:

*Dear* _____ *(the words "Dale Dougas" had been handwritten on this line),*

*At your request, we are returning the contribution you made to The Millennium Time Capsule in the final days of the last Millennium. We can understand your excitement at seeing once again this personal treasure you saw fit to preserve for posterity. The Committee hopes that its return brings you great pleasure in the years to come.*

*On behalf of the Committee and all the residents of Paisley, Washington, I would like to thank you for the contribution you made to preserving the history of our community and the memory of "the way we were".*

*Sincerely,*

*F. Abe Beals*

*Vice President (Community Outreach)*

*Pacific Verge Mall Corporation*

Dale turned the envelope over in his hands several times before opening it. He hadn't requested the return of his contribution. Indeed, he hadn't been aware that the time capsule was being opened. He didn't even know the mall was expanding – he hadn't been there since the adult video store relocated to a former pawn shop on Main Street. He went to the fridge, grabbed another Rainier, turned down the TV and began to read his own words, written a decade previously...

\*\*\*\*\*

My name is Dale Douglas, I am twenty years old and I have lived in Paisley, WA all my life. In celebration of the new Millennium, the town of Paisley has invited its citizens to contribute items to be placed in a time capsule that will be opened in the year 2049. What will actually happen when the time capsule is opened, no one seems sure, but it is hoped that many of those who contribute to the time capsule will still be around when it is opened. I hope that I am not. But in case I am, I decided I better think of something to stick in their stupid time capsule so that in 2049 I'm not the only person who gets nothing when it is opened.

I have decided to contribute this short written account of my life here in Paisley in the year 1999. I doubt it will be of interest to anyone, even myself, in the year 2049, but maybe if someone from the future reads this they may have a chuckle or two at my expense. Actually, knowing the people here in Paisley today, by the year 2049 everyone will have forgotten that there even was a time capsule, or else forgotten where they buried it. It probably won't be opened until the year 3049, when archaeologists discover it among the buried ruins of drive-thru restaurants and the calcified sludge lagoon behind the pulp mill. In which case, maybe this account of life in Paisley in 1999 might be of interest. [WARNING TO ARCHAEOLOGISTS IN THE YEAR 3049: Do NOT use this account of my life to make conclusions about everyday human life anywhere on Earth, not even Paisley. The ruined buildings and layers of petrified pulp-mill sludge which surround this time capsule were the accomplishments of other, more highly motivated individuals.]

First, a little something about myself and my upbringing, so that those reading this account can understand a little about what motivates me or, more to the point, why to others I appear to lack motivation entirely. As I said above, I am twenty years old and have lived in Paisley all my life. I have lived with my parents in the same house all my life. I have a younger brother, but we have so little in common I believe I may be the bastard son of a former mailman. Or maybe my brother is. My father works at the pulp mill, where he has worked every day since he finished high school in Oregon and moved up here looking for work. He has got "seniority", which enables him to impose his will upon twenty other guys on his shift at work, and on me when he gets home afterwards. My mother works part-time as a cashier at a supermarket. She and my father get along great, which means that I ought to get along great with my Dad, since I get along great with my mother, but I don't. I won't go into the reasons why, since this account is about me.

At the moment I am enrolled in the first year of a 3-year program in Applied Industrial Design and Technology at the local junior college, which was imaginatively named "Paisley College". The school's sports teams (of which I am not a part and won't be until surfing becomes a competitive junior college sport) have the nickname "The Fighting Scots", something I find amusing since I have never met a Scottish person in Paisley my whole life. Besides, I thought it was only the Irish who were "Fighting".

I will be dropping out of Paisley College at the end of this term, meaning that I will have nothing to do when January 1, 2000 rolls around. I figure that my parents will catch on somewhere around the third week of January that I am not going back to school, but that's no problem. I'll just tell them that the Y2K bug ate my college registration number, and that I have to sit out until I can re-register the following term. They might believe that – they heard about the Y2K bug on CNN.

I am not dropping out of Paisley College because I am stupid. My mid-term grades were pretty good, especially when you consider that I skipped about half the classes. And I have nothing against applied industrial design and technology, it is a useful thing for modern society to learn, especially if it is applied to environmental technologies that reduce pollution (I suggest starting with Paisley Pulp & Paper). I am more into ideas as opposed to applications, so I don't fit in well with this program. I took it mainly to get my parents off my back. Unlike kids who went off to bigger universities where there's parties and football games and things like that to do when you skip class, there's not much going on at Paisley College if you ditch. Campus consists of two nearly-windowless buildings of classrooms and faculty offices, a self-serve cafeteria, a big parking lot, a running track, and a soccer field.

Evergreen State is where I would prefer to be, because it has really good environment-related degree programs. Unfortunately my high school graduation scores and my SATs were OK, but not particularly good, and certainly not good enough to get into Evergreen. I don't think my grades accurately reflect my potential (one of the few thing on which my parents and I agree) but it is hard to achieve good scores when you are constantly being distracted by the ocean. Other than junior college, my only other options are going out of state (but who can afford out-of-state fees?) or Washington State. Wazzu is a good school, but it is on the eastern side of the mountains, in a spot that is geographically farther from the ocean than any other point in Washington. For a surfer, it's like Siberia.

I should explain my use of the term "surfer". I like to call myself a surfer, and by the standards around here I am one. However, western Washington is no Hawaii in either climate or size of the surf, so compared with those guys you see on ESPN2, I am not much of a surfer. In Hawaii, the native Hawaiian surfers refer to others as "howlies", a word that describes most people who surf near Paisley, and which is what I would be called if I ever showed my face in Hawaii.

Paisley is not on the ocean, but on a river, fifteen-point-three miles upstream from where it empties into a sheltered, reedy bay. For posterity I have given this specific location for Paisley in 1999 because, at the rate the river is being contaminated by factory farms upstream, the bay will probably be silted up and have waterfront condos built on it by the year 2049. Most kids in Paisley don't get to the ocean too often, which is sad since it is so close. But that is the mentality around here. Most kids would rather hang out at the mall or ride dirt bikes or just watch a lot of TV. I got hooked on going to the beach real young. I was lucky, when I was a kid a family from our neighborhood invited me every summer to join them on their holidays at the coast. When I was sixteen I was able to scrape together enough cash to buy myself an old pick-up truck, which I still drive, so that I could hit the beach whenever I wanted, which was most of the time.

As I said, it is hard to get good grades when the ocean is constantly distracting you. I never felt alive when I was sitting in class at high school. It was only when I was in my truck heading for the coast that I started to feel anything at all. Even in the middle of January, when the water is downright icy, I still like to go to the beach and hang out. I bring my tent and a few beers, catch up with some of the local guys and at night build a little fire. No matter when you go, every day at the coast is a new and different one.

That's the main reason why I've skipped so many classes at Paisley College. Some mornings when I get up for school, instead of heading east towards campus, my truck just seems to go west of its own accord and I end up at the coast. Fortunately my tent, surfboard, wetsuit, and cooler are always in the back of the truck.

Although I am only alone when I want to be, I think I'm becoming a bit of a loner. Not the kind of loner who mails bombs to corporate executives, don't get me wrong. I simply mean that I spend a lot of time alone in thoughts that I don't share with others. I don't have any particularly strong relationships on the go right now. I have my share of girl friends, but no one serious.

My best friend, Blake, who lived out at the 'Port, is now at UW. We used to hang out a lot before he moved to Seattle. I went up and visited him there last month. He likes living in the city, and doesn't come home except for Christmas and Easter.

Because Blake was gone, I spent a lot of time this past year surfing on my own. It's OK to be on your own, but sometimes when you get back to the sand you want someone to talk things over with, or to share a beer with you while you stare at the waves. Without Blake around, I act a little different at the beach. Especially in the July and August, when the Seattle and Tacoma people come down for their holidays, there's a lot of women at the beach, you can't help but notice them. When I was surfing with Blake or some of the other guys, I didn't pay so much attention to the women as I did when I was alone. I remember one time two summers ago I was walking out of the water with my board, I had just had a great ride, and when I got up to where Blake was sitting with our cooler, he asked me what she said to me. "She who?" I asked. He pointed out a girl walking off in the distance and said that as I was coming up the beach she went out of her way to walk near me and say something. Blake said I must have said something to her because she laughed, but I swear to this day I still don't recall having even seen that girl. I was still too buzzed from the ride.

Surfing on my own, this doesn't happen. In July I was stepping out of the water and a woman went out of her way to walk past me. This time I noticed her, and stopped to chat, and I invited her up to my cooler for a beer. She was from Bellevue, and had taken some time off to spend her fortieth birthday at coast. She was very pretty, and though I suppose I ought to have been uncomfortable about the difference in our ages, I wasn't, and she wasn't either. We got along well. A gentleman doesn't kiss and tell, so I won't, but I can say that we saw a lot of each other last summer. She told me there were things in her head she needed to sort out (i.e. memories of an ex-husband) and that the ocean helped with the process. We spent a lot of days and nights together on the beach, and this also seemed to help with her sorting. I haven't heard from her since September. She has gone back to her suburban world and moved on, and that's OK.

I should move on, too, but to what? I'm not sure. That's the way things stand here, in my life, at the tail end of 1999. It sounds corny (or worse, it sounds like my father speaking) but I hope that I will amount to something in the future, that my life will have some purpose. And even if that doesn't happen, I know that the ocean will always be there for me.

Happy future, everyone! Dale Douglas, November 24, 1999

*****

Dale Douglas was re-reading his letter from his younger self for the third time when he heard his wife drive up in the minivan, just back from a morning of shopping at the Pacific Verge Shopping Mall 'Time Capsule Days' Sidewalk Sale. He leapt from the couch, the beer spilling onto the floor. Instead of helping her bring in the shopping bags, he rushed past her, hopped behind the wheel and sped out of the subdivision, the rear door wide-open and spewing marked-down bags of "fun-size" Three Musketeers bars onto the street.

Dale drove the fifteen and three-quarter miles to the coast (the bay having already silted up forty-five hundredths of a mile this millennium), slowing only to roll down his window, shake his fist, and hurl a stream of unprintable obscenities at the Pacific Verge Mall as he passed. He stopped to rent a board and a wetsuit at the 'Port, and drove on to the break he surfed years before. As he paddled out, he thought to himself how he felt alive again, for the first time in many years. His mind was clear and pure as the first of the big waves crashed over him.

The coast guard officer who pulled Dale from the water the following day remarked that he had never recovered a drowned body with such a contented look on its face.

# Imagining #3: Twelve Pies

Al came to our town from Canada a few years back and opened a welding shop in the old building where the feed supply used to be. Although he tried to keep to himself, people took to him quickly. Each year he sponsored a little league team and always donated a good prize – usually football tickets – for the charity raffle held by the Women's League. For last year's Thanksgiving parade he and the guys from his shop made a float, the first real float our little parade ever had. They covered a flatbed trailer with white cotton "snow" and built a big Santa sleigh, with a deliberately broken runner. A couple of his guys pretended they were fixing the broken runner with their welding machines, and stuck July 4th sparklers in the end of their welding guns to make it look like they were really welding. On each side of the float hung a banner that read, "Don't worry Santa, we'll have it ready for Xmas".

We would nod 'hello' when we ran into one another at the diner as we took out cups of coffee, but I never got to know Al well until after one of my hunting trips up north. Driving home late one Sunday night, not long after crossing back over the border, the axel mount snapped on the trailer I was towing. There was not much I could do about it at the time, so I unhitched the trailer and left it at the side of the road, sticking my business card to it with duct tape. The next morning I drove over to Al's shop to see if he could send someone out to fix my trailer.

When I arrived at his welding shop, the big loading bay door was open. Five or six guys were working inside the shop. The nearest one was on the floor grinding the welds smooth on a big steel base of some kind. I waited until the sparks stopped flying and the fellow took a break, caught his attention and asked where I could find Al. He pointed over at two guys in coveralls who were cutting a length of steel in an iron-working machine. Both had their backs to me, and I could hear them talking loudly about football over the noise of the machine.

"Al, someone here to see you", called over the guy who had been grinding. The guy holding the back end of the steel angle nodded his head and shouted back, "OK, gimme a second". Once they finished cutting the angle, Al looked over, waved, and pointed to the office. We walked to a glassed-in booth overlooking the shop floor that contained two desks, one tidy, the other strewn with papers and technical drawings. Al handed me a paper cup of coffee and some cream and sugar packets, motioned me to the seat at the tidy desk and took his seat at the other.

"You're the county parole officer aren't you? What can I do for you?"

I told him my name and explained about the broken axel on my trailer. "No problem", he said, "I'll have Dave follow you in the truck and he'll fix. I should warn you, it might take him a couple tries to get it right, but don't worry. Even though he's still learning, he's a diligent kid and he won't leave you till he's done it right. I'd send someone else along with you but I'm a little short at the moment, my lead welder had a few too many at Trumps last night, it being his birthday".

"That'll be fine", I said. "What do I owe you?"

"You don't owe me anything. But I do know that Dave's sister is getting married next month and he'd like to get her something nice. Give him fifty bucks and we'll be even". With that, Al went out to the shop floor and gave instructions to an awkward-looking, pimply-faced teenager, who looked over at me and nodded seriously while Al was talking to him.

As Al was walking me out to my truck, a thought occurred to me. "I don't suppose you're looking for another welder, are you? I've got a guy coming out of detention next week and I'm pretty sure he's done some welding in the past." Al replied, "Yeah, sure, send him over, I'll see if I can find some work for him". He never asked why my client had been locked up.

The guy I sent over to him the following week did indeed know a little bit about welding, and ended up working for Al for over a year before moving on to a better paying job at Milkens, a big factory at the south end of the county. As the guy's parole officer, I had to go over to Al's to check up on his progress from time to time. As a result, I got to know Al a lot better, and together we soon began doing more for the public safety of this county than had been done in my previous twenty years of being a parole officer. Let me explain.

This county is not a very wealthy one, and the population has been declining for years. We're tucked up under the border, unnoticed by the rest of the country. Factory outlet malls are the county's biggest revenue-generator, with the rest of the "service sector" – that is, burger joints and gas stations – coming a distant second. A little farming still goes on, mostly berries and such, but most farmers gave up trying to compete with California boys years ago. The only industry we have of any note is Milkens, which is literally only a couple hundred yards on our side of the county line. That was done deliberately five years ago, when Milkens decided to build a new branch plant, because it allowed them to take advantage of the subsidies and tax breaks the state gives to companies that locate themselves in poor counties. Most of their workers commute up from counties to the south. They haven't created as many local jobs as they promised, and the company gets so may breaks our county doesn't see much in the way of revenues. Milkens sponsors a little league team, but it, too, is in the next county south.

The highest-level educational institution in our county is the one high school. Kids with any ambition have to leave, and when they do, they tend not to come back, except at Christmas. The kids that stay around here hope to get a job with the county services department, the only employer around here that pays a wage you can live on. The fast food joints and gas stations that line the interstate pay minimum wage and don't mind if they turn over employees every three months. Same with the outlet malls.

For people with time on their hands, there isn't much to do around here except watch TV or drink. The ones who are young and single drink over at Trumps, while the serious and seasoned drinkers cluster at George's. The kids who aren't yet twenty-one drink in their cars while their parents drink at home in front of their TVs. Some of the kids have started using harder drugs than booze or grass, but with a little luck I'll be retired before it gets too out of hand. With the young guys, being a big-time drinker is a badge of honor that is worn proudly and loudly. While earning that badge they get on a first-name basis with the county police, and eventually push their luck too far, too often. That's when they get to know me.

There's not much I can do to help a young guy the first time he gets put on probation. If he realizes he messed up and is going to go straight, he will do so without any help from me. Otherwise he will get himself back into trouble. He won't kill anyone – at least, not intentionally – but he'll get back to drinking and messing up until he winds up before the judge again and draws time.

When a guy gets released from his first brush with incarceration, that's my best chance to reach him. If there's an opportunity to go straight, most guys will take it. But finding that opportunity is not easy. The guy's got to get a decent job in fairly short order, but in case you didn't follow me the first time, there aren't many decent jobs in this county, especially not for guys just out of jail. I do my best to help him find work, but the most I can usually deliver is a minimum-wage job cleaning out grease traps at a burger joint, which no one ever sticks with for more than a couple weeks. I can't blame them. And so, too often the opportunity gets missed, and the guy slips into the spiral of poverty, alcoholism, and recidivism.

Al helped a lot of guys break this cycle. He would give a chance to anyone I referred. His answer was always the same when I called: "Send him over, I'll see if I can find work for him". Although not all of them worked out, most of them did. Al started them at fifty cents an hour over minimum, which doesn't sound like much, but the extra fifty cents was symbolic – it meant that the guy wasn't being treated like some teenager starting his first day making French fries. Al would tell them when they showed up on the first day that "the only way you can fuck up is if you don't understand how to do something and you fail to ask for help". Our community would be better off if more institutions adopted the same slogan.

Al treated his guys with respect. I would go over to his shop periodically to check up on my clients, and it would always please me to no end to see some guy working his ass off who a few weeks earlier had been sitting across my desk, hiding his vulnerability behind a mask of sullenness, arrogance, and suspicion. Al started them out on simple jobs that they couldn't really screw up, like running the drill press or working with the grinders. If a guy showed he was going to stick around, Al would train him on the welding machines. Not all his employees were ex-cons, of course. Many were just young guys seeking a job that taught them the skills to move on to something better. Most did move on. Al couldn't afford to pay even his best employees more than twelve-fifty an hour, and after a year or two a guy had learned enough from Al to get a job at Milkens', where they start welders at thirteen bucks an hour. Or they head to Seattle, where they can almost twenty.

After Al had taken on a few of my cases, I suggested that he apply for a subsidy the state gives employers who are willing to hire people just released from prison. "They'll pay you three dollars an hour for each guy you hire, for up to three months. I can put in the forms for you if you like."

Al said that he was reluctant to take the state's money, since he needed to hire workers anyhow, and my ex-cons worked harder than most for the wages he could offer.

"But you don't understand", I protested, "they're giving it away anyhow. Every burger chain out on the interstate takes it, billion-dollar corporations that certainly don't need it".

"If that's the case", he replied, "I'll take the subsidy. But don't get down on those guys who own the burger franchises, they're small businessmen, just like me. After they're done paying the rent and buying over-priced burger meat and cups and straws from the head office, they don't have much left over to pay their employees. The bigwigs at head office and the shareholders might be making big bucks, but the guy who runs the restaurant is often no better off than me. That said, I wouldn't help him out by eating the slop they serve in those joints. I stick to the diner, they make nice pies there."

After a couple years, Al's business grew and he had twelve guys working for him full-time, and he could still find work for one of my clients on short notice. Now, twelve jobs might not sound like much, but let me tell you, around this community twelve jobs count for a lot. That's twelve guys able to settle down, get married and buy a home. Twelve fewer drunks on a weeknight, twelve fewer cases for the county parole officer to worry about. Twelve more people with reasons to be hopeful about the future, twelve less who couldn't give a damn. Twelve extra pies sold at the diner. There's no community anywhere that doesn't need something like that.

For Al, however, the stress of having so many employees began to show. He told me once that, "...getting enough orders to keep this many guys busy isn't easy. Up till now I've been doing a lot of small contracts, but now I need to line up something bigger and steadier." Luck seemed to be with Al, because a few weeks later he won a contract to supply electric motor mounts to a big Tacoma-based company that made cranes for unloading ships. He now had enough work to keep a dozen guys working on a steady basis. Al had to lease some more equipment to get the contract, but it was worth it.

With this new contract, Al's business got so busy the old feed mill building was scarcely large enough to contain it. The local chamber of commerce started worrying that Al was doing so well he would soon pull up stakes and move closer to Seattle. They sent a delegation to sound him out on his future plans, but Al just laughed and handed them all paper cups of coffee and sugar and cream packets. He told them not to worry, he wasn't going anywhere, but hoped he could count on their support for his upcoming application for a permit to build an addition on to the old feed mill building.

I wish I could say that everyone lived happily ever after, but I'm afraid this story doesn't work out that way. Eighteen months after Al got that big Tacoma contract, Milkens decided to expand into the market for port equipment, and bought a big stake in the company Al was supplying. As part of the share purchase agreement, the Tacoma company agreed to buy its components from Milkens and nobody else. They cancelled their contract with Al with two weeks' notice.

This put Al straight out of business. Al tried to get a meeting with someone at Milkens to see if an arrangement could be made so he could keep making the motor mounts, but no one at Milkens returned his calls. I suggested to Al that he get a lawyer and sue for breach of contract, but he said, "That won't do much good. By the time I got my day in court I would still be out of business, and owing money to the lawyers on top."

"Well, I suppose then," I continued, "that you'll let go a few staff and get back to working on small contracts...?"

"Afraid that won't happen. I gave up a lot of my smaller customers when I took on that Tacoma contract, and the economy isn't as good as it was eighteen months ago, so getting them back or getting new ones is almost impossible. I'm low on working capital. No, I don't have any option left but to sell off my equipment and the building to pay off most of my debt. I'm leveraged pretty good. I'll probably have to sell my house as well, but fortunately I still have a place up north."

On the last day of work Al had the diner bring in a big farewell dinner for his guys. Al invited me to join them. The meal was served on the loading dock, on a couple tables pushed together to make one long one, with the big door wide open. We all sat along one side of the tables so we could look out at the late afternoon light, our backs to the shop floor. The guys who hadn't been with him long tried to make conversation while we were eating, and we smiled and laughed too loud at their jokes, and were grateful to them for their attempts to keep back the silence. After the meal, while we ate our dessert, Al thanked his dozen guys individually. He gave each of them an envelope of cash, the amount inside increasing with the length of time the guy had worked for him. Al told them to use it to buy something nice for their wives or girlfriends.

I never felt more ashamed.

Imagining #4: Wolves

Snow never fell that winter, not a flake, and many dogs died. Wolves came down the valley as they did every January, but found the lake unfrozen and their usual prey – herds of elk and deer – safely out of reach on the other side. Starving, the wolves began eating our dogs. The men would sit up at night, keeping watch with their shotguns. But the men would grow drowsy, and the wolves were patient and careful despite their hunger, and each morning more dogs were dead.

I remember that winter vividly still today, though I was then just a boy. My father and the other men took their revenge in the spring. They tracked the wolves back up into the hills, and burned their pups in their dens. The men repeated this every subsequent spring, even though the snow never again failed to come. By the time I was old enough to understand such things, no wolf could be found in that country.

My father hated wolves. This emotion was not unique among the men of our community. Once, when I was sixteen, I asked him if wolves did not have a right to live in the hills, so long as they never harmed people. This question had come to my mind while reading a report in our local newspaper that a wolf had been hit by a truck out on the highway, although the conservation officer assured the public the remains were those of an overly big coyote. My father flew into a rage. Spit sprayed from his mouth as he recalled the deaths of the dogs that long ago winter, how it was a miracle none of the children were attacked, and how the government should never have cancelled the wolf bounty back in the seventies. As he raged, I dared not speak the thoughts running through my mind: That the wolves came near town only because they were starving. That the dogs were easily killed because they were chained out in the back yards. That the wolves never came near the doors of the houses, and never in daylight, when the children were outside. That starving men in the Yukon killed and ate their dogs when necessary. That our town's most celebrated wolf hunters had been men of no account, shiftless ones that never kept a proper job. I kept these thoughts to myself until his fury ebbed, and I withdrew, while he returned to his TV show, muttering.

After high school I left home for college, the first in my family line to do so. For reasons unrelated to wolves, my father and I could no longer speak more than a few civil words to one another. I adopted wolves as my battle-standard for the war between us. The walls of my dorm room I decorated with prints of wolves peering at the camera from behind trees, and with poor quality posters of blue and gray airbrushed wolves howling at overly large, overly cratered, yeast-colored moons. I purchased recordings of instrumental music overdubbed with wolf calls from a store that sold New Age goods like incense and hemp clothing. I didn't listen to them often. I dated a Salish girl for a time, mostly because my immature mind somehow connected her Indian-ness with wolves, even though she was born in the city and had never seen wolves other than the ones on my walls. After college I ranged far from my father's home, and seldom called.

My father is now an old man, and suffers from an illness for which little can be done. The reasons we had for turning on one another as younger men have been forgotten. I would now like to visit him more often than I do, but I must care for my own children and for the people who work for me.

The town into which I was born and where he still lives has changed greatly. New people came and bought up many of the older houses, people who were raised in other places. They chuckle at the old-timers and their tales of long-dead dogs. In the hills above town the government has begun re-introducing wolves with the encouragement of the new people. The wolves are brought from forests far away, where they have never known a snowless winter.

My father's memory of wolves is now hidden away in a part of his mind from which it is rarely recalled, although I know it is still there. He rarely leaves his house. His strength has declined rapidly in recent months, and he now remains silent for long stretches of time. I doubt he will live past spring. A nurse comes to visit him most days. He was given a pager which he can use to call for help when needed, but he won't wear it. He says if things get so bad he's tempted to use it, he doesn't want it handy. He would rather die alone than in the care of strangers. When I visit we sit out back if the weather allows. His eyes seldom venture beyond the yard, but mine are drawn to the hills in the distance, where they search for signs of wolves. I have yet to see any, but I am grateful that they have been returned. I would not like to think that, come spring, this country would be left to the coyotes.

# Imagining #5: Glacier, WA

Sunday morning smothered Waterloo in a thick blanket of snow that overwhelmed the city's fleet of snow ploughs, closed the streets, and allowed residents to return to bed after a moment's glance out a window. I had a quick cup of instant coffee, took my skis and poles from the laundry room, and walked out through the garage door. I stretched briefly in the driveway, snapped on the bindings, and skied to Adam's place through the deserted streets. Leaving my skis outside his door, I rang the bell and followed him up the long flight of stairs to his apartment condo. The building had once been a private school for girls, and had sat vacant for many years until a developer bought and converted it to its present purpose. Adam occupied a portion of the top two floors. The weak light filtering in through the snow-covered skylights colored the room blue-grey. 'I refuse to use electric lights in the daytime', he said, lighting a large beeswax candle and setting it on the coffee table. Waving me to a seat, Adam tossed over the bag of cookies that had been his breakfast, turned down the Miles Davis music, and began explaining why he had summoned me from my warm bed so early on such a wintry day. But before I begin to recount what he said, I'll share a few details about Adam, so that his story does not seem more unusual than it inevitably will.

Adam and I met in university, in Montreal. He was in business school, specializing in management information systems; I was a geography major. He needed to take some easy electives – 'bird courses' – outside his program to boost his overall grade point average, and thought he'd take Geography 101, an intro course for non-geography students. Unfortunately, he misread the prospectus and enrolled in Geography 100, the mandatory course for geography majors. Instead of the "coloring maps for credits" course he hoped for, Adam found himself wrestling with geomorphology, hydrology, adiabatic lapse rates, and the like. As often happens, by chance we selected lecture seats next to one another the first day of class, connected, and started hanging out. Montreal is the coolest city on the continent, and how we managed to get good grades while making the rounds on Rue St-

Denis, I'm still not sure. In any event, we've been friends ever since, even though our careers took us in different directions.

After getting a Bachelor degree and then a Masters in geography, I did several consecutive six-month contracts for various government ministries in Toronto, a city about 1% as cool as Montreal, carrying out environmental impact assessments. After a few years of this, I came to Waterloo to work on a PhD, which I'm still doing. It has taken longer than I expected, since I continue to accept the odd government contract and sacrifice a semester of research by doing so. But it's how I can afford to maintain a mostly student-like existence while still owning a house of my own.

Adam survived his unexpected brush with physical geography, and after university started working as a management information systems specialist, just as the field was about to take off. He bounced around several large high-tech companies that sold mainframes, decided in the early 1990s that small, flexible networks based on this newfangled internet-thing were the way to go, and set himself up as a consultant for small companies that thought similarly. He joined a Waterloo start-up, and moved here. Adam was good at what he did, and so were his colleagues at that start-up, and they are now all of them wealthy and retired from the company. He no longer needs to work, and so chooses only projects that interest him.

Neither of us have ever had many long-term romances. I've always had a number of female friends, some of which I slept with, as grad students often do, but I've never had anything you'd call a serious relationship. Adam was really serious about a girl he met immediately after university, but that ended after only a couple months for reasons long forgotten or never known. In recent years, when word of Adam's financial success spread, he attracted plenty of interest from potential romantic partners, but the right one never seemed to come along.

Once we were reunited in Waterloo, Adam and I would meet for beers at Ethel's most Thursdays and, when our schedules permitted, take off for a few days of backpacking or canoeing in summer, skiing or snowshoeing in winter. Neither of us is obsessed with any one particular activity, we're kind of outdoor generalists, we'll try anything so long as it's outside. Our circle of friends includes mostly like-minded people, so even when we haven't planned something together, we often find ourselves meeting up in a group of people at a trailhead somewhere.

So now you know a bit about what we're like.

Skiing to Adam's that snowy morning, it occurred to me that I hadn't seen much of him in the past year. I don't know if I'd seen him more than once or twice in the last eight months, and I hadn't been aware he was back in town. I knew he'd been spending a lot of time out west in Washington state, working with a Microsoft subcontractor, but that's about all I knew. My PhD supervisor had been getting on my case to knuckle down and do some field research, so I'd been up in northern Ontario as much as I'd been at home. All this to say, I was eager to catch up with Adam, but puzzled why he needed me to come over right away, in such weather.

So, as I munched away on cookies, Adam began to talk...

'Thanks for coming over, Zack. I should have called sooner and let you know I've been back in town for over three weeks now, but I haven't been in touch with anyone. I needed some time to myself to think, and now that I'm done thinking, I need to tell you what I'm about to do.

Remember I went out to Washington a year ago last fall to work for that Microsoft subcontractor? Easiest money I've made yet. I know you're no techhie so I'll spare you the details, but let's just say they needed someone to help them meet an impossible deadline and I was the guy they needed. It was stuff I'd done a dozen times before. If you calculate what I charged them on an hourly rate, it was robbery. Most of what I did was simply checking code written by their guys. I'd rattle off some fixes and suggestions, and send it to them overnight. I only needed to be on site once a week for a production team meeting, and even that seemed like overkill, but if that's what the customer wants, that's what they get.

I'd been to Seattle a couple dozen times already, so after putting up for a few days in one of those suite hotels. I figured I might as well get a change of scenery, maybe find a place somewhere nearby in the mountains, where I could get a cabin and do some hiking or snowboarding when I wasn't working. I was in REI and mentioned this to one of their staff who, it turned out, is a big-time backpacker. He suggested I try finding a cabin near Mt Baker. Baker's a big mountain north of Seattle, surrounded by national forest. It's closer to Vancouver than Seattle, but it's still an easy drive down to Seattle for meetings. He said that although Baker gets the most snow of any mountain on the coast, the runs are never crowded because everyone from Vancouver goes up to Whistler, and most day-trippers from Seattle head east to Snoqualmie Pass. During the week, he figured I'd have the place to myself.

So the next day I drove north to Bellingham on I-5, then east on 542 out to Baker. There's nowhere to stay on Baker because, like I said, it's in a national forest. The closest place is a little town called Glacier, just outside the forest boundary. It isn't much – a few houses, general store, snowboard shop, trailer park, and a bunch of cabins. They had a roadhouse bar, but it burned down not long after I arrived. It has a surprisingly good little Italian restaurant, but its main attribute is being the closest place to Baker to rent a cabin. The guy at REI was right. Even on weekends during ski season the place is pretty quiet and, during the week, quieter still. Just what I was looking for.

Just off the highway east of Glacier I found exactly what I was looking for, practically the last cabin before the forest boundary. It's about a hundred yards back from the road, the only cabin on this dirt track. The landowner had wanted to develop a dozen or so fancier condos along this track, but he ran into financial problems, and this one cabin was all he'd been able to build so far. It wasn't a palace, but it had everything – water, electricity, and phone, plus a wood stove, desk, and a bed.

My first few weeks there fell at the tail end of a beautiful autumn. The forest is mainly spruce and fir and cedar, but there are enough alders and birch to give it a blast of color in the fall. Most days I hiked the mapped trails in the area, getting a feel for the place. I would get up early, hike until mid-afternoon, then put in a couple hours of work based on what my client's staff had coded that day. I'd cook for myself most nights, a pot of soup or something like that...'

At this point I interjected, 'Adam, why are you telling me about what you cooked for supper? Substitute a tent for the cabin and maples for fir trees and it sounds like any number of trips you and I have done here in Ontario'

'That's exactly my point', said Adam, continuing his narrative. 'I need you to see that everything was totally normal, it was just the same old me when I got to Glacier. So as I was saying...

I spent the fall hiking in the national forest. Winter came early last year; it was the year after an El Niño, and once it started snowing late in September, it didn't stop until spring. The resort opened earlier than ever. The hiking trails were a mess for a week, but pretty quickly there was enough snow up the valley from Glacier to need snowshoes or skis. I had both with me. So my routine became a couple days snowboarding, a couple snowshoeing or cross-country skiing, a day in Seattle to check in with the guys who were paying my way, then a down day to read or go into town for a paper, a meal at the Italian place or a couple beers at the bar. Occasionally I needed to spend a full day working, but not often. And though I wasn't trying to be a recluse or anything, I didn't make any effort to have anyone out to my cabin.

I spent Christmas with friends up in Vancouver, but only stayed a couple days, anxious to get back to my little cabin in the woods. I picked up some winter camping gear in Van so I could do some overnight hikes in the mountains. When the weather was willing, I could get way into the backcountry where there wasn't any chance of seeing another living soul.

Or so I thought. On my second overnighter in early January, I skied up a small river valley to the north of Baker. About three in the afternoon I was keeping my eyes peeled for a place to camp, and came upon a partial clearing that looked promising. When I got closer, I saw that the snow was beaten down by human tracks, and that someone had built a winter camp there. It wasn't a cabin, more like a big lean-to frame with fir and spruce boughs dragged up all around it, cedar spread on the ground and, as I learned later, a tent in the center. There was a small trail of smoke coming from what looked like a kitchen area, enclosed on exposed sides by more spruce boughs, and overhung by an old conifer. Snow had drifted up high on two sides of the enclosure.

I had heard the stories of Free-men – white supremacists, end-of-the-world nuts and the like – who live in the mountains of Washington state, but they tend to be farther east, towards Idaho. Besides, this camp was too isolated and too small to be home for more than one or two people. I stood wondering what to do. I mean, you don't expect normal people to be living out there in the backcountry, do you? I thought about either moving on or turning back, but the day was getting late, it was starting to snow, I was tired, and wherever I went I would have to camp within an easy walk from this spot. Because it hadn't snowed that day, nor was it likely to, my tracks would easily be seen. So, if there was a lunatic living there, he would have no trouble finding me. I knew I wouldn't be able to sleep a wink just thinking about it.

My decision was made for me. Just as I was summoning up the courage to approach the camp, a kid – I am not making this up – a kid, who could not have been much more than four years old, came out of the camp. He spotted me, and came towards me yelling 'Daddy, Daddy'. He stopped a few yards short and, realizing that whoever I was, I wasn't his daddy, he turned back and ran. When he got within a few steps of the shelter, a woman came out of the darkness and pushed him inside.

She stood and faced me, looking calm and confident.

I wasn't calm or confident, but I pretended like I was. I took a few steps toward her, so I wouldn't be shouting, and stopped. I said, 'hi', the same way I did when I walked into the store in Glacier for the first time, to the woman standing in front of the cigarettes. 'Hope I'm not troubling you. I was just hiking up the valley here and couldn't help but run into your camp. I didn't know you were here. I hope you don't mind'. Once my words were spoken, the only sound above my breath and my heartbeat was the patter of snowflakes on my Gore-Tex jacket.

She looked at me with a set chin and asked if I worked for the Forest Service. When I reassured her that I didn't, that I was just an overnight hiker passing through by chance, she appeared to relax, and asked if I wanted a mug of tea before heading on my way. Although I didn't really have time to stop if I was going to find a place to camp for the night, there was no way I was going to pass up the chance to find out who she was and what she was about.

The woman turned to re-enter the shelter, pausing slightly in mid-step and motioning me to come in. I followed. I guess I took off my pack and my skis – I mean, obviously I did – but I don't remember doing so. What I do remember next is stopping in the entrance, expecting to need a few seconds to allow my eyes to adjust to darkness, but it was surprisingly bright inside. The moments that passed while she made the tea and handed me a mug were silent. Taking the first sip from her own mug she glanced up at me and said, as matter of factly as if we were old friends meeting at the Italian restaurant in Glacier – and I know it must sound ridiculous, but I swear it's true – she said, 'It's good to see you'.

I didn't know what to say. I was dumbfounded. I swear I had never set eyes on her before, and yet there she was, talking to me like she knew I was coming. You must be thinking, was she nuts? After all, why else would she be living in the middle of nowhere, with a kid, and behave that way when meeting a stranger. Shouldn't she be afraid of me? Hesitant? Something? But no, she wasn't. She was calm, cool, composed. I was the one behaving strangely, standing there speechless.

Sipping my tea, I studied the room around me as I tried to think of something to say. I saw that the shelter had started as a tent pitched on solid ground, around which had been constructed a framework of poles cut from nearby conifers. Evergreen boughs were hung over this to form sloping walls. It was difficult to tell if the roof was a man-made rigging of boughs, or simply the overhanging limbs of a large spruce. I later found it was a mixture of both, with a tarp woven in but mostly hidden. The floor was not muddy, as might have been expected, but was carpeted with thick, well-trodden layers of boughs.

Whoever built it – I assumed she did – knew what she was doing. A fire pit lay off to one side. The ashes that rose when she stirred the coals floated straight up and out through a gap in the overhanging limbs. A rough, low, handmade table crouched near the fire, surrounded by logs that served as stools. Some pots and cooking utensils and a few belongings hung from the poles. Against some logs a large pile of boughs was heaped and covered with a blanket. I later discovered this formed a very comfortable place to sit, as comfortable as any couch.

The temperature inside the shelter was warm enough to be comfortable without a jacket. Winters on the west side of the Cascades rarely hold the dry, bone-crushing cold of the eastern slopes. They're mild and damp, and the fire had taken care of that. What struck me most was that, unlike other small human habitations, there was no smell. Well, I shouldn't say there was no smell at all; rather, the air inside was fresh, with the smell of the fire mingling with the background scent of the conifers.

Another thing which occurred to me in those first few moments – and of course, it has taken me much longer to describe my initial observations than it took to make them – was that there was no mirror...'

'Were you afraid she was a vampire?' I interrupted. I was starting to feel a little uneasy about Adam's story, and how intense he was getting while telling it. But he was not fazed, and continued:

'No, no, don't be silly. I was puzzled by how she could look so clean, so presentable, so... good, without the benefit of a mirror. I found out later that she had a separate sleeping place a little farther back in the woods, which makes sense, since you wouldn't want to sleep where you eat in bear country. She didn't wait for me to speak, she just went ahead and asked about my day's journey: where I had come from, how the trail had been, wasn't the snow beautiful that day, and so on. I answered as best I could, speaking in broken sentences, and with too much nervously loud laughter. Not like me at all. She told me I didn't have to stand, and motioned me to the log seats near the table. As we continued our small talk, I was able to look at her more carefully, although I noticed she was not studying me as intently as I studied her.

She was probably in her mid thirties, with fair skin and the freckles and faint lines and wrinkles of someone who spent a lot of time outdoors. Her hair was auburn with wisps of gray, neatly pulled back and tied with a bit of brown yarn. She had good teeth and a small smile that she flashed a lot. Her nose was a bit too small for her face, but then, you probably aren't interested in what her nose looked like. When I had first seen her standing in the clearing, I saw that she was tall and lanky but athletic. She was no ballroom beauty, but in those wool pants, hiking boots, a plain sweater and scarf she was wearing, she looked perfect enough to me.

I took my time sipping the tea, still uncertain what to say or do next. I was starting to enjoy the sensation that I was being treated like a long-gone friend, by someone who had missed me while I was away. It was getting late, and if I was to find my own camp for the night, I really needed to get moving – if I wasn't too late already. Up to that point, our conversation had been composed mostly of small-talk, the stuff that long-married couples exchange over dinner at the end of a long working day, assuming they live in the back woods. She must have recognized what I was thinking, because she said that it was getting late and that I wouldn't find another decent campsite before nightfall, so why not pitch my tent near her shelter?

Her suggestion elated me. I got up, my movements suddenly easy, in contrast with the awkwardness I had felt since I arrived, and in a few minutes my camp was set up a respectable but close distance from hers. I took out my provisions for the night and brought them back to the cooking area, where she had started working on dinner. She was making some rice and I suggested we could add my...'

'Adam, man, enough with the Martha Stewart shit. I don't care what you ate or what you talked about over tea. Who is she? What was her name? What was she doing there? Get *on* with it.'

'Sorry, Zack, I was just getting lost in my own story. Anyhow...

To answer your questions, simplest first, her name is Ava. She was born and raised in northern California. I should point out that it took several hours that evening, and all the next day, for me to learn what I am now telling you about her. Whenever I tried to ask her a direct question about herself, she would answer as if she was providing me additional details about things I already knew about her.

She grew up in that way Californians think is normal but sounds weird to the rest of us. Raised in Santa-something-or-other by what she described simply as 'nice' parents. In high school she was selected as being 'gifted' and was placed in a program where she and the other gifted kids were allowed to create their own curriculum, study whatever the hell they wanted. She learned nothing, but was given good grades, and went on to environmental studies at Humboldt State in Arcata. Ava spent several years after college doing the kind of work that you are always doing, Zack. Measuring forests, setting up plans for monitoring fish populations and so on. She told me she got tired of doing it, though; tired of the paperwork and constant need to work a network of people in order to get her next contract.'

'I can relate', I said.

'I bet. Anyhow, five years ago, she met a guy who worked for the forest service – or maybe it was the parks service? I can't recall which. In any event, he was transferred up to Washington shortly thereafter, and convinced her to come with him. He wasn't from the coast; I think she told me he was originally from Nevada or somewhere like that. Anyhow, he was a big time back-country skier, who was sent to Washington to do avalanche control work in the winter, and some mapping and fire monitoring in the summer. They spent their summers camping in areas where he was working, and in winter they usually rented a cabin somewhere on the edge of the Cascades. They had a baby their first summer in Washington. It was an unexpected gift, Ava said, and made her very happy.

I don't know much about her relationship with this other guy. I don't even know his name, she never used it. She never spoke poorly of him, but she never spoke fondly of him either. Just matter-of-factly. What I do know is that about eighteen months ago he got promoted and was transferred to Washington DC. Ava had no desire to leave Washington state, and he left her there with some money and their child. He still deposits money into her bank account each month.

It had been several years since Ava had left California, and she told me how she had come to love the tranquility of the North Cascades. One night we spent together, Ava spent several hours describing to me in simple, beautiful terms her feelings for the mountains. If I tried repeating to you what she said to me, you'd think she was a flake, like one of those silly granola women who sell beads at Grateful Dead concerts. But there wasn't contrived hipness or Earth Mother shit on her part. She had simply grown to feel at home there, and was able to express her feelings more articulately than anyone else I've ever met.

No doubt you want to know why she was living in the mountains by herself last winter. That's the heart of the matter, Zack, and why I asked you to come over here today.

As I said earlier, that first afternoon I stumbled across her camp, Ava let me set up camp next to hers. The three of us had dinner together that night, and she and I talked for hours like old friends. Her son pretended to read, but most of the time he was watching me out of the corner of his eyes until he fell asleep. When we were done talking, she said good night and carried him off to her sleeping shelter back in the woods. When I woke up the next morning – in my own tent, of course – I pulled myself together and then walked over to her main shelter. Ava was already up and dressed, and had made breakfast. She was still talkative, but was now asking a lot of questions about me. Not the sort of questions you would ask if you're just getting to know someone – you know, like, where are you from, where did you go to school, etc – but more like, what projects I was presently working on, what my schedule was like, and so on. As I keep saying, it was as if in her mind we already knew each other, and that she was trying to update herself on recent developments in my life.

Ava invited me to camp with them another night. I was up to date with my work, so I could afford to spend another night away from the cabin without any worries. Even had I been behind schedule with work, I still would have stayed on. She was fascinating. We spent the day doing chores around the camp. They weren't onerous, and I took my time doing them because I was enjoying myself. I played a little with her son. Seemed like a good kid, didn't say too much. I felt a little sorry for him living up there with no other kids around, but it didn't seem to be doing him any harm.

That evening, after her son was asleep, I sat with Ava near the fire and we continued our day-long conversation which, by this point, had moved on to the state of public education in Washington, rural poverty – I can't remember what all we talked about. Earlier in the day, when she started talking about modern societal issues, I started to think maybe she was in the mountains hiding from something. You know, maybe she had been a victim of violence, or was one of those Y2K-type wackos expecting an imminent apocalypse of some sort. But no, the more she spoke, the more I realized that she was as level-headed as you or me, and that there hadn't been any traumatic experiences to drive her into hiding. It was clear that she did not consider what she was doing to be 'hiding' at all. Her choice to live up in the backcountry was as normal as mine to live in Glacier.

When we both started to fade that night, Ava told me that, if I wanted, I should feel free to come back up to her camp and visit again. She touched my shoulder briefly as she stood up. Her body language said it was time for me to go back to my own tent, which I did. Next morning I got up early, packed my tent, had a quick mug of tea with Ava – she was always up early – and skied back down the valley. Although it took me several hours, the time flew past, my feet hardly touched the snow, and I was in Glacier before I knew it. As I descended my mind poured over every detail of the time I had spent with her.

The following morning I received a frantic call from my client saying they needed an urgent fix for part of their system I hadn't worked on before, and could I come to Seattle right away? I did, and ended up staying the next three nights in a hotel. But while I was working, while I was driving down the interstate, while I was falling off to sleep in the evenings, all I was really doing was thinking about was Ava.

When I finally got back to my cabin in Glacier, I found it had snowed again while I was away. I packed my stuff that night and made an early start in the morning, the weather being good. I had no trouble following my previous route, and made a pretty good pace, worrying the whole way that Ava wouldn't be there when I arrived.

But she was there, just like before. This time she had seen me coming from a little farther off, and had the tea ready when I arrived. She gave me that same smile of hers, and said she was glad to see me again. I gave her some supplies I had picked up for her, not sure if she actually needed them. She laughed and made a fuss about receiving them, as if I'd just returned from India with a cargo of tea and spices, instead of from the PCC in Fremont with a sack of oats and quinoa.

This, then, became my routine. I would spend two nights up at Ava's camp, ski back down to Glacier, work for a couple days, visit my client in Seattle for a day, then return to Glacier and ski back up to Ava's. Only the occasional emergency on the part of my client or a really foul snowstorm interrupted this routine. I forgot about snowboarding. And the whole time I was away from her camp, I thought only about returning to Ava and her mountains. I...'

'Adam, I hate to interrupt to ask this. You know I'm normally not so crude – or at least, I haven't been since we left university – but I have to know, were you screwing her?'

Adam laughed when I said this, and seemed to relax a little more. I on the other hand had become increasingly intrigued and somewhat agitated as his story unfolded. By this time, he had been talking continuously for almost an hour, but Adam looked as though he could go on indefinitely. Although I was now thirsty and hungry – the cookies having long disappeared – I didn't want to interrupt him any more than I already had, until my increasing preoccupation with whether he actually had sex with Ava got the best of me.

'No, we never had sex', Adam continued. 'Don't get me wrong, though, I would have done so gladly. I thought she was beautiful, the most beautiful person I've ever met. Everything about her was, to me, perfect, inside and out. No, she never made the offer, and I enjoyed being with her so much that I never raised the issue. Whenever I stayed there, I always set up camp next to hers, and always slept in my own tent at the end of the day.

Thinking back on it, she probably would have slept with me if I had suggested it, but I never did.

It was early last March when everything came crashing down around me. I was in the final stage of my project, and was having to work well into the night at my cabin in Glacier in order to free up days to spend with Ava. The weather had turned warm; trails at the lower end of the valley were getting sloppy, and each time I went up to her place, it took longer. Although I didn't know it would be our last time together, one night at her camp I raised with her the question of the future. Our future. She started talking about the past instead, and I'll now try my best to tell you as closely as possible what she said to me:

"You have never asked me directly the reason why I have been staying here alone in the mountains nor why, that day when you first arrived here, I was not afraid of you. The reason is simple – or at least, to me, it is simple. When my son's father was preparing to leave for DC, I spent a lot of time reflecting on my past. I saw that I had spent most of my life searching for something, without knowing what it was I was searching for. There is nothing unique in this; people often say things like this, and some who say it really mean it. Since the day I first saw them, I have loved the North Cascades, and this valley is one of my favorite places. So before he left, I asked him to help me build this camp, so that I could continue to stay here for a time.

Once I was alone, I came to understand that there was nothing left for me to search for. I could identify no one particular thing – apart from my son, whom I adore – that I had attained or obtained which brought my search to an end. Motherhood, spirituality, finding a place you want to call home, overcoming the physical tests of the elements – looking back now I am sure that, cumulatively, these were the things that had been the subject of my search. But at the moment I received each of these gifts, I was not aware of the significance at the time.

No longer needing to search for anyone or anything, I discovered that, instead, I wanted or needed to be the object of another's search. And so that is why I continued to stay here in this valley, in these mountains. Only here could I be found by another, if I was prepared to wait. Which is what I did.

And then you came. A few other people came up the valley before you, last autumn, but none stopped. When winter came, I didn't expect to see many people, if any at all, but I wasn't concerned. I suppose if the months had begun to stretch out indefinitely I might have questioned the wisdom of my decision, but it didn't matter once you came.

You will recall that, when you first arrived, I asked if you worked for the Forest Service. I knew you didn't, but I still needed to ask and see how you responded. I saw at that instant that you were the one who was looking for me. And although you didn't realize it at the time, that is why you came, and why you are here with me now."

Ava had taken my hand and held it while she was speaking. And when she finished, she squeezed it ever so lightly, smiled, collected her sleeping son, and went off to bed.

I am not sure how much longer I remained where we had been sitting together. I suppose it wasn't more than a few moments. I got up and went back to my own tent. You might think I would have been sleepless that night. But I wasn't. I slept soundly, soundly.

The next morning I woke early, had tea with Ava, and left for Glacier.

When I returned to my cabin, I resumed work as usual. The following morning, I got yet another panic call from my client. I won't bore you with the details, but something had gone horribly wrong with the first dry run of their finished product. One of their most trusted system engineers wasn't so trustworthy after all, and quit the company, leaving a mess behind. I had to spend the next ten days in Seattle cleaning it up. Needless to say, I charged them an outrageous fortune, not just because I could, but because they kept me away from Ava.

When I finally got back to Glacier it was too late in the day to head into the mountains, though I wanted to. I packed my gear and went to bed early. The next morning I set out before it was light, eager to get to Ava's camp. It was a tough slog; the weather had fluctuated wildly in the past ten days, alternating between warm sunshine and heavy dumps of wet snow, making the trail an absolute mess.

When I got to the clearing, Ava was gone. The poles and boughs were still there beneath the conifers, but her tent and belongings were gone. No disaster had struck; it had clearly been an orderly departure. What with the weather, there was no way of telling how long she and her son had been gone nor where they went. There was no note. She didn't need to leave one, I knew why she had left.

I didn't bother staying at the clearing more than a few moments before returning to Glacier. I asked a few questions at the general store and, sure enough, the clerk there told me that a woman and child had been in the store about a week ago, and told him they had spent most of the winter camped out past Baker. The woman had mentioned she was looking forward to when the North Cascades Highway reopened so they could make a summer camp in the high country. As to where they were going in the meantime, she didn't say.

Each day last spring was the longest day of my life. I had to spend way too much time in Seattle with my client, and was constantly on the verge of exploding with frustration. When I had a free day, I would haunt the towns and villages of northwest Washington looking for Ava. I didn't think she would have gone to Seattle. I went over to the Olympic peninsula a couple times to look for her. I even flew down to Arcata and hiked around the redwood forests for a few days, hoping maybe she had gone back there for the spring.

My work in Seattle finally finished a week or two before the North Cascades highway reopened. As soon as it was, I was up in the high Cascades searching for Ava. At the outset I looked frantically, in an explosion of energy and activity. As summer wore on, the sense of urgency dissipated and was replaced by a doggedness. I moved up one valley and down the next – they're almost infinite in number, or so it seems, and Ava could have been camped in any one. And I am certain she was. She had deliberately left just enough information for me at the general store in Glacier for me to know where to look.

My search was fruitless. The guy who runs a fly fishing shop east of Twisp thought maybe he'd seen her camped up Central Creek, but I found no trace of her there. Snow comes early to that part of the country, and I had to leave with the closure of the highway. I returned to Glacier, where I had kept the cabin throughout summer. My first day back I went into the general store. The clerk told me that a woman with a child had been asking for me there less than two weeks previously. She had asked the clerk to tell me, if I came in, "thanks". She hadn't seen her since.

And so, Zack', said Adam, clearing his dry throat, going to the kitchen and returning with a beer for each of us, for it was getting close to noon, 'to bring a long story to an end, that is why I asked you to come here today. I bought the cabin, along with all the property along the dirt track, so that mine will continue to be the only cabin there. The last several weeks I've made all the arrangements to sell this place here in Waterloo. I won't be working any more. I've got plenty of money, it will be many years before I will need to work again, if at all. I'm going back to Glacier.'

'Let me get this straight, Adam. You are packing it all in to spend the rest of your life, or at least, the foreseeable future, chasing after Ava? Even though you don't know where she is, nor where she'll be? Simply because she hopes you will?'

'Well, it's not simply because she wants me to, but, yes, that's what I plan to do.'

"That, my friend, is pretty fucking cool."

*****

I spent another thirty or forty minutes at Adam's place. We had another beer and talked about the logistics of wrapping up his life here in Waterloo and setting up in Glacier permanently. By the time I left it was afternoon, and the good citizens of Waterloo had begun taking to the streets, safe in the knowledge that schools and work places – save the coffee shops and the Princess Cinema – were truly closed for the day. I clipped my feet into the bindings, and pushed gently off with my poles, making my way home through the snowy streets without any particular sense of urgency, ignoring the drones of snow blowers being fired up in the driveways. I thought about Adam and his Ava. And I saw that both of them, not just Ava, were getting what they wanted. Ava had said that she wanted, or perhaps needed, to be sought, and she is now comfortable in the knowledge that Adam is out there, constant in his search for her.

And as for Adam, he too has found what he wanted. The first time he met her, she made him feel as though he was a long-away traveler returning home to someone who thought about him while he was gone, and who was pleased at his return. That is a powerful feeling, probably the most powerful one that a man can have, though it's one I myself have never experienced. But Adam has, and he knows that at the end of each day he spends looking for her, Ava and her mountains will be waiting for him.

Authors' note: "The Time Capsule" was first published in the now-defunct online literary journal, *The Dragonfly Review*, in 2001. That beautiful journal, published out of San Juan Island, was ahead of its time.